THEY CALL HIM SKINNER

Timothy James Riley

This book is a work of fiction. Names, characters, places and incidents are either the product of the author's imagination or are used fictitiously, and any resemblance to actual persons, living or dead, events or locales is entirely coincidental.

They Call Him Skinner

Edited by Elegant Editing, Los Angeles, CA

Cover: Photo Courtesy of Library of Congress: Lewis W. Hine Collection

ISBN: 197614051X
ISBN 13: 9781976140518
Library of Congress Control Number: 2017914289
CreateSpace Independent Publishing Platform
North Charleston, South Carolina

I dedicate this book to the three people
who helped make it happen:

My wife Penny – her patience was endless
My sister Jeannine – she refused to let me give up
My teacher Bonnie – if only I had been a better student

CHAPTER ONE

This time, they waited until he was almost finished before coming for him and his precious piece of the sidewalk.

He glanced at the 20-foot high clock across the street on the corner in front of the Wells Fargo Bank and noticed it wasn't even five o'clock. He'd sold all but three of his 200 newspapers more than an hour earlier than normal and that meant a quick dip in the creek before supper. He dragged a faded red bandanna out of his back pocket and wiped the sweat off his forehead as he watched the wealthy business men move from one office to another.

At 15, he was the youngest to ever win and hold the city's prized location for selling newspapers. The northwest corner of Madison and Main was as close to a gold mine as any working-class kid in 1920 Butte, Montana was ever going to get. But this valuable location came at a cost. Black eyes and bloody noses, busted knuckles and jagged cuts, endless scrapes and deep bruises were given and received as he constantly defended his 10 square feet of sidewalk. The pain could last for days, but in the end, when he counted the money he had earned, the reward was worth it all.

Suddenly, he heard the familiar voices deep inside his mind: *They're right behind you. Three of them. Turn to your left.*

"Get your paper here. Big fight comin'," he yelled as if nothing was wrong. "World Champ Dempsey takes on anyone. Get your..." He dropped his newspapers, turned quickly to his left and blocked a blow to his face with an open hand. His counter punch connected squarely on the other boy's jaw and sent a jagged piece of white tooth flying. The kid dropped to the ground with a soft thud.

"Grab him," yelled the one on his right, but the kid was too slow. He threw a straight hard blow just below the chin and deep into a soft, vulnerable throat. The boy's eyes bulged as he tried to cry out, but there was no sound. His knees collapsed, and he squirmed along the ground searching for his voice and his next breath. Neither came and he quickly collapsed flat on his chest.

The last one was huge, maybe six or seven inches taller and at least fifty pounds heavier. The boy moved toward him in a slow, plodding cadence with fists raised high, talking all the way.

"Didn't need no help anyways. This is gonna be my corner. My money. I'm the one they'll all be talking about tomorrow. Not some skinny Irish kid who finally got his ass whipped."

He looked past his opponent's overwhelming size and focused on his one apparent weakness. The nose. Like a narrow one lane mountain road, it traveled down his face with sharp turns to the left and right before coming to a dead end just above his upper lip. It begged to be punched.

The boys circled to their right, then stopped and traded blows. He took a painful glancing shot on his left cheekbone and felt the skin tear just below his eye. He countered with a vicious overhand right that zeroed in on the boy's long, pointed nose. It broke instantly. Thick, dark red blood sprayed on his faded blue denim shirt and the fight was over.

He waited for a minute or so and then asked, "You boys okay?" Their beating had been swift, yet clearly painful. Finally, one of them managed to spit out a muffled, "Yeah."

"We done here?" he asked.

The same boy replied with another, "Yeah."

That's all he said. There was no threat of a next time or a possible rematch. They, like many others, had challenged Skinner O'Brien and lost. Their retreat was measured and filled with obvious pain.

He returned to his corner and quickly sold the rest of his papers. As he did, he silently thanked the strange little voices for their helpful warnings. Without them, he knew he would have lost some of the many fights he'd won over the last two years. With them, he was undefeated and much to his dismay, quickly becoming a local legend.

CHAPTER TWO

If they lined up every student in his two-story ten room, red brick school—all 147—and asked them how they felt about today, he was almost sure none would feel the way he did about the next three months without any school: he wished it wasn't going to happen.

In just over a minute, the clock over the doorway would strike twelve and in less time than it took him to finish his half-a-cheese sandwich, every classroom at the Sherman Public School would be deserted. It was a last-day-of-school tradition for first graders to eighth graders from the east side to join the other schools in Butte and race down to nearby Silver Bow Creek for an afternoon of fun and games. This was generally a good time for all, but he wasn't sure he'd make the trip again this year

His family had moved here almost four years ago from central California in August of 1916. They had just lost their peach farm to a rare, late spring freeze and his father hoped Butte's famous copper mines would be a quick solution to their money problems. But that hadn't happened and now, with each passing year, the after-school gathering became less and less a celebration and more a grim reminder he was still stuck here in in this miserable place called by many "The Richest Hill on Earth."

What a joke that was, he thought.

Sure, Butte boasted a population nearing 60,000, with more than 100 working copper mines, and 50 thriving saloons with names like Bucket of Blood, Frozen Inn, The Cesspool, Graveyard, and Pay Day. It was also a popular stopping point between the East Coast and San Francisco for many of the days' biggest celebrities, including President Teddy Roosevelt, Buffalo Bill Cody, and Mark Twain. Most importantly, it was America's number one source for much-needed copper, having pumped out millions and millions of dollars of the precious metal every year for the last 20 years. But for every ounce of the green rock his father and the thousands of other miners carved out of the tunnels below, someone was getting sick or hurt or even dying. Yet with so many men coming from every corner of the world, all willing—even eager—to ignore the sickness and dangers just to have a steady job in America, the streets and alleyways of Butte were filled with those who didn't or couldn't carry their own weight.

Drunks, bums, thieves, and prostitutes numbered in the thousands and posed a real threat to anyone caught in the wrong part of the city after dark. And yet, as Father often said, the true danger in Butte was hiding in plain sight behind a three-piece suit, starched white shirt, and newly shined shoes. These dandies were the mine owners and they were every bit as deadly as the thugs waiting in the alley shadows to steal your watch or snatch your pocket book.

It was a miserable place to live and he hated almost everything about it. Almost. The two exceptions were his school and a short, stocky Italian friend he met in class two years earlier. The kid went by the nickname of Sordi—it rhymed with "sore eye" and was often used by others because of all his fighting. They were best friends within a week.

As for school, it was an adventure, filled with excitement and an endless series of mysteries just waiting to be solved if you read enough books or asked the right questions. School was his magic carpet that took him away from this terrible city and off to the wondrous places he hoped to visit one day. School was the one thing that was safe and secure from the sickness and death that surrounded the current center of his world.

School was also Mrs. Camp, his teacher, his advisor, and his good friend, though she was anything but a kind and gentle soul. He'd been her student for all four years and he had loved every minute.

He didn't know much about her life away from his classroom, except what his mother was willing to share after one of her many parent-teacher meetings. That amounted to the fact she was unmarried and lived with a younger brother who suffered from too much whiskey, far too often.

"James Michael O'Brien."

When she used all three names he knew he was in deep trouble.

"Yes ma'am?" he replied.

As she shuffled her plump, pear-shaped body towards his desk in the back row near the large open window on the west wall, he watched his best friend and fellow gang member Sordi, disappear into the hall, the last student to leave.

"James, what's that on your face?" she asked.

"Just a scratch, ma'am."

"Another fight?" she asked.

"Yes, ma'am."

"Oh, James. What am I going to do with you?" she sighed. "What are you going to do with you? You're too old to still be fighting. At 15, the boys are so much bigger and just plain cruel. They can and will hurt you badly."

"I can take care of myself," he said and just stared at the ground.

"James, you're a special student and clearly a fine young man. I've never run across anyone quite like you in my 34 years of teaching," she began. "On the one hand, you're like a sponge soaking up every bit of knowledge and information that comes near you. You'll try any subject and other than math, you're always one of the best. You also have a deep, sincere concern for others and their well-being. Yet I hear from students and adults alike you can and do change into a mean, vicious fighter, who seems to revel in an endless string of victories."

"I do fight ma'am and, yes, it appears I win more than I lose," he finally managed to say. "But I swear on my mother's life, I hate fighting. I have never, ever, started a fight. And I never will."

"That's not enough," she snapped. "If you keep fighting, for whatever reason, chances are you won't last another year." Then, she surprised him by adding, "Such a waste of a beautiful mind and spirit."

He stood and took a step towards the door. She reached out, grabbed his hand, and said, "Wait, I have something for you." She handed him a small, dark brown book, thick with dog-eared pages and a worn and weathered cover of soft leather.

He carefully inspected it from front to back and then raised it to his nose, sniffing the cover. "Smells like smoke," he said.

"My father loved to read late at night by the fireplace," she replied.

"Your father? This book belonged to your father?" He glanced at the inside front cover and found a dedication: *From William Albert Camp, to my beloved son, Donald Macy Camp, 1854.*

"It was one of his favorites," she replied softly.

A detailed picture formed in his mind of an old man hunched over the book, his small, round spectacles reflecting the flickering light from the nearby fire. Then he turned the blank first page and read the title aloud, "*The Last of the Mohicans*, by J. Fennimore Cooper."

He knew she liked him. He really liked her too. But giving him a book that belonged to her father? "Are you sure you want me to have this?"

"It's time for you to go. Take the book," she said. "Maybe you'll read it over the summer and Lord willing, you and the book will return this fall."

"Thanks, Mrs. Camp. I promise to take good care of it."

"Promise me you'll also take good care of yourself too. Please James, not so many fights this summer. Use your mind, not your fists."

"I promise I'll try," he said, knowing Butte would give him little or no chance to avoid those looking to take his prized corner or add another notch on their victory belts. As she started to turn and walk back to her desk, he said, "Ma'am, may I ask you a question?"

She stopped and turned to face him. "Of course."

"Why won't you call me Skinner? Everyone else does."

"It's a badge of honor that reinforces and rewards your brutal actions," she replied staring straight into his eyes. "And you seem to wear it proudly."

"It's just a nickname. It doesn't mean a thing." He glanced out the window and away from her piercing glare.

"It means either you or your opponent ended up bleeding from who knows where and I won't condone that kind of behavior," Mrs. Camp said. "Does your mother use that name?"

"No ma'am."

"I wouldn't think so. Now go." She dismissed him with a wave of her hand and headed back to her desk.

He opened the book to the first chapter and wandered out into the hall. By the time he'd climbed down the two flights of stairs and out onto the schoolyard, he was already lost in the colonial wars of 19th century North America.

"Hey, Skinner, where you been?" yelled Sordi. "We gotta get going if we want a spot near the water."

"Ah, I was just talking to Mrs. Camp about next year's class." He began to walk in the opposite direction.

"Hey, aren't you going down to the Bow?"

"No, not this time. Got some things to do at home before I pick up my papers," he answered. "Tell the others I'll meet up with them at the loading dock around 3:30." After reading the first few pages of his new book, he'd made the easy decision to spend time with it and not a bunch of screaming little first and second grade kids.

Even so, he knew the Silver Bow was always a big event for most students in this part of Butte. Hundreds from the three public and three parochial schools would spend the day swimming, playing baseball, and eating huge picnic lunches. And generally, the unspoken truce against fighting was honored by the many gangs from Parrot Flats, Hungry Hill, Corktown and Dublin Gulch. That was not the case last year

A tall, heavy-set, 15-year-old bully named Bruno Dominici, had shown up with his gang from the tougher south side of Butte searching for fresh meat. They boasted about beating all-comers down there for the past year and made it clear they were out looking to expand their territory in this direction. After pounding on a couple of the smaller gangs from one of the parochial schools nearby, they moved on without any further confrontations. He didn't give their threat much thought. For us, fighting was still an accepted alternative to the more traditional sports of baseball and football.

Yet, in an especially bloody fight just last week, Bruno had sent a message with the leader of the losing gang that he was back and looking for a piece of the kid called Skinner.

CHAPTER THREE

The trip along the narrow, winding trail from school to home normally took 15 to 20 minutes without snow. Today, he did it in ten. This was his first book in over a month, and he was already hooked on the new adventure. He went straight through the tiny kitchen to the steps outside the back door, where he found his favorite spot and was soon reading about the main character's latest quest. He knew he only had a couple of hours before it was time to pick up his newspapers for the afternoon edition.

"Jimmy? You here?" asked his sister.

"I'm out on the back steps, Jessie" he yelled.

"What are you reading this time?" she asked and snatched the book from his hands.

"Hey. Be careful with that," he said. "It's a gift from Mrs. Camp."

After a quick look at the book, she handed it back and sat beside him on the top step. "Sure were lots of kids down at the Bow, today. You should have come."

"I had better things to do." He held up the book directly in front of her face.

"No. You should have been there," his sister said and stared back into his eyes. "That Bruno kid showed up with his gang. He told everyone you were a coward and afraid to fight him."

He continued to look at his book, but stopped reading.

"Did you hear me Jimmy? He called you a coward," she said, this time raising her voice as she leaned in towards him.

"I heard," he snapped. "Anyone get hurt?"

"What do you care? You have your stupid book." She jumped down off the steps, then turned back facing him.

"Did anyone we know get hurt?" he asked again.

"They picked on some of the German boys from Parrot Flats," his sister answered. "Beat them up pretty good."

"Where were Sordi and others?" he asked.

"On the other side of the creek playing kick ball with the gang from Meaderville. They never saw anything."

"What time is it?" he asked, as he marked his place in the book.

"What time is it? What time is it?" his sister mocked. "Don't you care about what this Bruno kid is saying about you?" Don't you care that he and his gang are looking for you? Don't you care about anything but your stupid books?"

"Yeah," he answered. "Right now, I care about what time it is. I need to be down at the Daily Post by 3:30. Now what time is it, Jessie?"

"Almost three," she blurted out, then stomped up the stairs and back into the house.

He jumped to his feet and followed her into the house. Quickly, but carefully, he placed the book at the head of his cot, hiding it under his pillow. Then he ran out the front door and down the hill towards the loading dock. It would take all of thirty minutes to cover the three miles over to the southwest side of Butte. He could do it. He'd done it before, but not being early at the docks would put him at the back of the line, and that meant trouble might be waiting for him by the time he arrived at his corner.

Two summers ago, he had finally reached the required age of thirteen to sell newspapers downtown. Gus Photopoulus, the foreman at the Daily Post, a big bellied man with a shiny bald head and a thick, bushy black mustache that completely hid his top lip, had decided to take a chance on what he called "the scrawny Irish kid" from Dublin Gulch. He warned him he had to sell fifty papers every day or he'd lose his job as fast as he got it.

At first, it took him more than three hours to get rid of his stack of fifty. All the other kids sold more than a hundred in less than two. Tired of eating a cold supper and earning only pennies for all his hard work, he finally got up the nerve to ask one of the others how he finished so soon each day.

"You need to get closer to downtown," replied a short, fat kid with torn, dirty overalls, standing in front of him waiting for his stack of papers. "You have one of the worst corners around, boy. No people. No sales."

The next day he made a point of getting to the loading dock early so he could grab his papers first and then stake out a corner closer to Main Street. Gus had told him every corner was open to the first one who got there. What he had forgotten to tell him was you had to fight to keep your corner.

At his new location, he sold a dozen papers in less than 15 minutes. He was feeling pretty good about his new spot when something told him to turn around quickly.

"What the hell you doin' on my corner, jackass?" said the tall, thin kid with long curly, red hair hanging down to his shoulders.

"I got here first," he replied.

The boy quickly threw a roundhouse punch with his right hand.

Skinner didn't know how or why, but he knew the boy was going to do that and pulled his head back and out the way just in time. Then he did the only thing he knew how to do. He dove at the kid's legs and knocked him flat on his back. The boy's head smashed into the cement sidewalk with a thud. The kid didn't move for a few moments and he was afraid he had killed him. When the boy finally began to move, he was so grateful he asked," You okay, kid?"

The boy slowly moved to a sitting position and rubbed the back of his head. "Yeah, I'm all right."

Not knowing what to do next and anxious for this to be over, he said, "We done here?"

"Yeah," the boy replied, as he staggered to his feet, rubbing the back of his head.

Still not sure what he was doing, he offered to shake the boy's hand. Apparently surprised by the gesture, the boy hesitated for a moment, then shook it and walked off.

That night at the supper table, he couldn't wait to tell his father what had happened. Certain his mother wouldn't be very happy, he decided to wait until after supper when his father was alone and sitting in his rocker on the front porch.

"Father? I'd like to talk to you. Alone."

"What's on your mind, son?"

"I had my first fight today."

"Oh?" his father said without looking up.

"I didn't start it," he offered up quickly.

"You all right, James?" his father asked, this time looking up at him.

"Yes."

"Was the other boy okay?" his father asked.

"Said he was," he answered. "When he finally stood up, I didn't know what to do next, so I offered to shake his hand."

"That was a good thing," his father said. "So, what did you learn from today?"

"I don't rightly know," he began. "It happened too fast for me to be scared. Then, when it was over, I felt bad for the other boy. He was just trying to protect his corner so he could sell his papers."

"You going to give up the corner tomorrow?"

"No sir," he answered quickly. "We need the money to get back to California as soon as we can."

His father, Sam, was a large man, over six feet tall, with huge muscled arms, broad, thick shoulders, and massive calloused hands. According to his stories, he'd been in many fights in his life and made it clear that fighting was a part of growing up for most young boys. It seemed especially important to Irish boys and their fathers. Yet for his father, it wasn't necessarily a part of being a good man. He made it clear Butte was nothing like their hometown of Fowler, California in the fertile San Joaquin Valley.

"Fact is son, Butte's not like any place I've ever been," his father advised. "Fighting here, in one way or another, is a big part of surviving for everyone."

"So, I'll probably have to fight again?" he asked.

"Most likely," his father admitted.

"So, what do I do? How do I win?" he asked and kneeled down to look his father in the eyes.

"I'll show you a few basic punches that'll help with most fights," his father said. "But winning isn't always about being the best boxer. Every kid you fight will know how to do that."

He waited for his father to continue speaking, but it looked like he was thinking of something far away. Finally, he asked again, "So, how do I win, Father?"

"First off, don't fight until you have no other way out," his father began. "Second, when you do fight, fight with all you have to win as fast as possible. It's better for you and your opponent."

"That's it?" he asked. "That's all the help you have for me?"

His father reached out his huge right hand and placed it on his son's left arm. He squeezed slightly, then said, "First off, don't ever be so afraid you back down. You're not going to die in a fight at your age. Even the worst beating will heal in a few days. A week at the most. Your honor is with you your whole life." His father stared down at the knuckles on his own right hand and then continued.

"It's fear that makes you feel the pain. Makes you hesitate. Forces you to quit."

"Did you ever quit?"

"Never."

"Did you ever lose a fight?"

"Sure. Eventually, everyone loses a fight or two," his father replied. "There's no shame in losing if you give it all you have. There's only shame in being a coward."

Then his father showed him how to stand, how to circle one way and then the other, and how to bend his knees to avoid most punches. He showed him how to cover his face and body from his opponents' blows. He showed him how to throw straight, powerful punches with his shoulder, instead of wild swinging, roundhouse blows that looked good, but rarely hit their mark with any real force.

With the lesson over for the night, he added one last piece of advice as they turned to enter the house. "Son, most kids don't want to fight. They're hoping to bluff you into backing down and running away. By standing your ground, you already have the advantage. Then, if you're strong enough to take a punch or two and not give up, I guarantee you'll win most fights that come your way."

"Father, there's something else I need to tell you," he started. "I don't know how, but I knew that boy was gonna try to hit me with his right hand before he made a single move. A little voice inside my head told me. I swear I heard it."

"Son, for more than a thousand years, the Irish people have been fighting off invaders from all over Europe," his father said. "Fighting is part of our heritage, part of our soul. Men, women, young or old, they all learned to fight for what was theirs and what they believed in. So, if fighting seems to come naturally, or you find you're getting pretty good, you can thank your ancestors for helping prepare you for the challenges you're facing today."

"But I don't want to fight," he replied quickly.

"Wanting and doing are two different animals," his father answered. "I don't want to work in those miserable mines. But I do. And thankfully, I'm damn good at it."

He wanted to believe his father, but with so many Irish kids among his victories, he didn't think this was the right answer.

CHAPTER FOUR

He proudly counted the day's receipts into the pale blue Maxwell coffee can next to his bed. Even though he'd been a little late in getting to his prized corner this afternoon, no one else was there and it had been another good day for selling newspapers. Seemed everyone in Butte wanted to read about Jack Dempsey, the new heavyweight-boxing champion of the world. He was coming to town in just three days for a big money exhibition fight. That kind of news meant the tips were larger than normal and came far more often. He was grateful for his temporary good fortune.

After a quick clean-up and brief inspection of his still-swollen face from Thursday's defense of his corner, he took his seat at the supper table. As usual, it didn't take long for his sister to start in on his fighting.

"Looks like the cut is getting worse," his sister sneered.

"It's not so bad," he replied quickly.

"Sure looks bad," she continued, this time loudly enough so their parents would easily overhear.

"Jessie, we all talked about this last night," he snapped. "Now please leave it alone."

From that first fight two years ago, he soon realized his mother could spot the slightest cut or bruise the moment he walked through the front door. He didn't know how she did it, but she always knew. Yet she rarely said a word unless the damage was more than he could hide.

"You ready to eat, Sam?" his mother yelled to his father, who was sitting in his favorite rocker on the front porch.

"That I am, Kathryn my love," his father replied as he strode into the room and took his usual place at the head of the table.

His family was like many stuck in Butte, struggling every day to survive and make a meager living. It was a hard life, with little time for play and even less energy for family bonding. Supper was the one event where his and many other families came together to share with one another. This was not an ethnic practice limited to just the Irish. His non-Irish friends often talked about the evening meal as a time when the family spoke about their faith and the hope for something better.

When it came to religion in their home, his father told them he had been a Catholic growing up, but no longer followed any organized faith. It was one of those subjects he would not allow anyone—friend or family—to discuss at their supper table. While not forbidden, he rarely spoke about his childhood or his parents. He had shared a few things over the years, such as he was a first-generation Irishman, born near San Francisco in 1885. His father Joseph was only two years old in 1852 when his parents, Patrick and Bridget, packed him up and left their beloved home in County Cork, Ireland. They fled to escape what the Irish called The Great Hunger that had already lasted for seven years, with more than one million Irish dead of starvation when their primary source of food—the potato—was mostly killed off by a disease. Additionally, another million Irish left Ireland in the mid-1800s, mainly for America. As soon as Joseph's family landed in New York, they joined thousands of other immigrants heading for California and the promise of a new beginning with the gold rush. Joseph's father was no miner, but he was a skilled woodworker, and soon made a good home for their family of three in a small town near San Francisco. For reasons Joseph never knew, his parents decided to not have any more children. While that decision didn't sit well with Father O'Sullivan at their local Catholic church, there would be no brothers or sisters in Joseph's future. Still, his childhood was filled with happiness and good fortune throughout his early years.

Choosing not to follow in his father's footsteps because he had no woodworking skills, Joseph studied finance at the university and entered the world of banking after he completed his education in 1875. In 1880, he married his college sweetheart, Sheryl Elaine Howe, and in 1885, they had their only child, a son named Samuel.

Sam remembered his parents always holding hands when they walked, laughing aloud for no apparent reason, and openly kissing each other—and him—no matter where they were. There were day trips to the beach and three or four-day camping trips in the nearby mountains. His mother often spoke about her childhood and growing up in the nearby San Joaquin Valley. Her family raised cattle and grew huge fields of wheat and alfalfa in the small town of Madera. She often used the evening meal to make a case for moving back and raising their son in a place where people cared for one another. Unfortunately, with the success of his father's banking career in San Francisco, it was always going to be "someday." That day never came when a tragic accident took his mother's life in 1895. From then on, the laughter stopped. The trips to the beach and camping stopped. And, his father's love and affection seemed to disappear almost overnight. Making matters worse, his loving grandparents decided to return home to Ireland to enjoy their final years around family and friends. Their departure from

Sam's life left him no other choice; he spent less time in the house, less time at church, and more time on the streets with the older boys from his school. It was there he learned how to protect himself and how to survive. Eventually, at the age of 18, he left home the day he finished school, traveling to his mother's hometown of Madera to start a new life. He hadn't seen or spoken to his father since that day and he made it clear to all that he had no plans to ever see him again.

Skinner's mother, Kathryn, who was raised in a loving home until she left for nursing school at age 18, was the softer side of the family. She was always the peacemaker, and often acted as referee in discussions and arguments between her husband and her teenage son. Unlike his father, his mother loved to talk about her family and her years as a child growing up in the Midwest.

Kathryn's mother, a full-blooded Cherokee, whose name Ayita meant 'first to dance', was 18 and living on a reservation with her parents in Oklahoma when she first met her future husband. Colonel Jonathon Francis Chamness, of the U.S. Cavalry, had been stationed at Fort Gibson in north-eastern Oklahoma and was charged with keeping a watchful eye on the local tribes. It was on one of his regularly scheduled visits that he met and immediately fell in love with Ayita, telling everyone who would listen, it was not only her beauty, but her free and open spirit that took him prisoner for life. However, while a marriage between a Native American woman and a white man was clearly legal in the late 1800s, it was openly frowned upon by both sides. They didn't care and were married within a month. Soon after, Jonathon resigned his commission with the U.S. Cavalry and joined the Texas Rangers. They moved to Emory, Texas, just outside Dallas, and added three girls to their happy family, with Kathryn being the first in 1885.

Life for the Chamness family in Texas was more than good, as her father's career brought him many citations, promotions, and ever-increasing compensation. The only drawback was the time he had to spend away, leaving her mother to raise the three daughters.

She did so by combining the good from each heritage, especially the Cherokees' love and respect for nature and the animals around them. They would often spend a summer night outside and away from the house, to feel closer to and safer with their surroundings. Now here in Butte, with Sam's view of traditional religion as a big waste of time and energy, she turned to her father's spiritual lessons as the basis for a guiding belief in some power greater than themselves. It was a good life and one she longed to share with her two children before they left home.

These stories of his parents' childhood often filled the boy with thoughts of what 'could be', instead of 'what was' being stuck in Butte. His father worked ten hours or more, six days a week in the local mines. His mother, whom he had heard many people say was a pleasant-looking woman who wore her Cherokee heritage well, worked a full eight hours the same six days in a hospital laundry. Even his 13-year-old sister Jessie worked part-time for a local veterinarian. Every member of his family knew they were here for only one reason: save the required $5,750 down payment for their California farm as quickly as possible. After four years of scrimping, saving, and hoarding every penny, nickel, and dime, they had put away some forty-five hundred dollars. Almost a thousand of those hard-earned dollars had come from his paper sales and he was proud of his contribution.

"With school out for the summer, you'll be starting up with the morning papers tomorrow?" his father asked.

"Got to be at the loading dock by 6:00," he replied. "With Dempsey coming to town, I could make an extra two or three dollars between the two editions, if the sales continue like today."

"If you survive tomorrow you might," his mother added, her voice filled with uncharacteristic anger.

"Might not have to fight if I get there first," he said.

"James, you have one of best spots in Butte for selling newspapers and everyone knows it," his mother shouted back. "Seems there's always someone looking to take it for themselves. Not everyone is afraid of fighting another skinny Irish kid."

"He better be a pretty good fighter if he wants my corner," he replied firmly.

"Your corner?" his mother snapped.

His father put a temporary end to the squabble by announcing it was time to eat. His mother seemed to calm down a bit and offered a short prayer of thanks. He silently added his gratitude for what they had before them, meager as it was.

Tonight's meal was unusually quiet as the tension between him and his mother was still near the surface. When they were almost finished, his father attempted to change the mood.

"We've had a pretty good week," his father announced. "What with James bringing home some extra money from his afternoon papers and Jessie learning she'll be allowed to work pretty much full time this summer."

"I wouldn't be earning those dollars if I didn't fight for the best corner," he mumbled, but loudly enough for all to hear.

"Well son, the money will do us no good with you lying dead in some alleyway, now will it?" his mother answered sharply.

"Enough. That's enough," shouted his father. "I'll not have that kind of bickering in my home. I had enough of that with my father, him blaming me and me blaming him for my mother's death when I was just 10 years old. How sad a thing that such a minor accident as a fall down a few icy steps would take my mother's life and cause a loving father to stop loving his son forever."

"Sam, please," his mother pleaded. "No need to bring those painful memories up again."

"No, my love, but each of us needs to be reminded that our words are every bit as damaging as the most powerful blows ever thrown," his father said. "My father's constant jabs and digs over time forced me from the home I loved and the father I cared for with all my heart. A father I've neither seen nor heard from since I left almost 18 years ago."

"Mother, I'm sorry for raising my voice to you," he said.

"James, you know I love you and only want the best for you," his mother replied. "I wouldn't hurt you for anything. And I don't want anyone else hurting you either."

"You're right. Tomorrow's likely to end up in a fight," he said. "Win or lose, I promise I'll be careful." Then he reached across the table, held her hand and wondered just how badly tomorrow's fight would be.

CHAPTER FIVE

Mornings began at five a.m., every day of the year for each member of his family, except his sister. For whatever reason, she treasured sleep more than any person he had ever known. It didn't matter in the least if it was eight degrees or 80 in their small sleeping area, she was always the last to get out of bed to leave for school, work or even just a fun day.

Today was Saturday, the beginning of summer vacation and the first day he'd be selling the morning edition. From the middle of September until the third week of June, school would limit him to afternoon paper sales and the meager profits it could provide.

"Morning, mother," he said. He sat quickly and gulped the glass of cold milk. Then he worked on the small bowl of cooked oats and some toast.

"Morning, son," his mother replied softly.

"Mother, I'm sorry for last night."

"James, I've thought it over and I've decided to believe in you, instead of worrying about you. Between your mind and your fighting skills, I trust you'll do just fine," she replied.

He continued eating and thought about last summer's challenge to regain his morning corner. It had gone much easier than he had imagined. A big German kid standing almost six feet tall, with huge, calloused hands and bulging biceps had firmly settled in and was busy selling papers. Yet despite his impressive size, he soon proved to be no fighter. All it had taken were a couple quick jabs to an unprotected nose and the first sight of blood sent him on his way. Skinner hoped for a similar occurrence this year.

There were several routes he liked to take down the hill and across town to the loading dock. Each took little more than 30 minutes and was an easy hike. Today, he decided on the alleyway between Copper and Brawley streets. He was enjoying the fresh, cool air as the sun broke over the Boulder Mountains in the east, not really paying much attention to anything in particular. As he approached the end of the alleyway and the cross-street Washington, six boys ran out in front of him, blocking his path.

"Good morning, fellas," he announced, offering a broad faced smile as he came to a quick stop about ten feet away.

No one in the line spoke. No one in the line smiled.

He eyed each boy up and down and by the time he had removed his cap, stuffed it into his back pocket and readied for a fight, he knew there was only one who might give him real trouble. He took a step towards the boy and then stopped. Something wasn't right. He suddenly knew he wasn't going to fight this kid. It was Bruno he was going to meet today. He slowly turned to see another boy, maybe a few inches taller and much heavier, standing some 10 feet away.

He wore a black work shirt, black pants, and a black conductor's cap, pushed back on his head. His had a dark, ruddy, sickly look about him. His face was large with a squared off protruding jaw and a long-jagged scar running across the right side of his face from his nose to his ear. The boy asked, "You Skinner?"

Before he answered, a new piece of information filled his head and he started to smile. "Hello, Bruno. Or should I just call you Ronnie? Ronnie Dominici?"

"What the hell? How did you know that name? We never met before," Bruno asked, clearly unsettled.

"Let's just say a little voice told me," he answered.

"Listen up, punk. My name's Bruno. Just Bruno. The last kid who called me Ronnie still can't see so good out of one eye."

"Sure wouldn't want that to happen," he said with a big smile. "I just love to read. Maybe I'll have to put a whippin' on you instead."

"You don't look so tough to me," Bruno yelled back. "When I'm done with you, they'll be calling you 'Skinned', instead of Skinner."

The gang laughed and soon began yelling chants of "Bruno. Bruno. Bruno" as the big kid started to circle slowly to his right.

"I'm not looking for any trouble," Skinner said. "I'm just headed to the Standard to pick up my papers." He knew there'd be no way to talk his way out of this one. But this little talk wasn't meant to dissuade Bruno from fighting. It was meant to give him more time to watch this big kid's movements and maybe spot a weakness or two.

"I got your papers right here punk," Bruno said as he moved forward, throwing a roundhouse punch that missed by several inches, but was quickly followed by a short, powerful left hook that did connect on his right eye, knocking him back against the wall.

Smiling broadly, he said, "Nice punch, Bruno."

"There's plenty more where that came from," Bruno taunted, as he paraded around in front of his gang.

"Not sure I want anymore," he replied as his vision cleared and his resolve set in.

Bruno moved in to finish him, but he had celebrated his advantage a little too long and the fight was back on. By the time Bruno had lumbered across the six or seven feet between the two fighters, Skinner had swiftly moved to his left and delivered a sharp right cross on Bruno's left eye. The boy's knees flexed as the punch cut a deep gash into a vulnerable, unguarded, bushy eyebrow.

"Lucky punch, kid," Bruno said as he straightened and moved back a step. He wiped the blood from his face, took a deep breath and threw off his jacket.

"There's plenty more where that came from," Skinner replied, mocking Bruno's earlier remark, and taunting him into making another mistake by stepping in close enough for a stinging left and right hook combination into his unprotected ribcage.

Again, Bruno's knees buckled, this time taking him to a squatting position, his hand and arm clearly straining to hold his massive body off the ground. He reached to wipe the oozing blood from his blinded left eye and cringed openly. It would have been easy for him to approach unnoticed from Bruno's left side and deliver another punishing blow as his opponent struggled to catch his breath and clear his vision. But that wasn't the way he fought. He gave most every opponent the time they needed to regain their feet, before he continued the battle.

"You ready to call this off?" he asked Bruno. "I will if you will!"

After a long pause, Bruno straightened back up and moved towards him saying, "I'll call it off when you're on the ground, bleeding and unconscious."

Bruno moved in towards him and raised his hands to signal the fight was still on. Yet instead of throwing a punch, Bruno kicked his large, black work boot deep into his stomach, knocking him back and doubling him over as he tried to catch the wind that had apparently been knocked out of him.

"How's that for calling it off, punk?" Bruno howled and then moved in for the finishing blows.

At just over five feet tall and a slender, supple physique, he was far too agile for the large, lumbering fighter. He stayed just out of range as he remained doubled over, pretending to help his lungs refill with much-needed oxygen. The kick had hurt him some, but not nearly as much as it appeared.

In the previous exchange, he had hurt Bruno and they each knew it. He also knew Bruno was a brawler and would use any trick he could think of to win the fight. While most kids never thought to use their feet, he had fought a few who would—especially the French kids. In its best form, foot-fighting could be a very effective weapon. But that required speed and flexibility, and Bruno had neither.

Bruno cocked his big right hand and moved in to deliver a crushing blow to his injured opponent. As he did, Skinner exploded upward with a devastating uppercut, delivered precisely on the end of Bruno's rugged, square jaw. This fight was over before the last of Bruno's collapsing body hit the ground.

For several moments, the boy lay still, knocked out cold by the vicious blow. He backed away, watching and waiting for some sign of movement. Finally, there came a soft moan, followed by a hand reaching up to rub a bright red chin. As Bruno continued to recover, Skinner glanced over at the other boys, making sure they wouldn't try to even the score. No one moved an inch.

When Bruno had managed to push himself back to a sitting position, he walked over and asked, "You okay?"

Bruno paused for a bit. Then he replied," Yeah."

As soon as Bruno was standing, Skinner walked over, offered his hand, and asked, "We done here?"

Bruno ignored the hand and replied, "Yeah, we're done. This time."

CHAPTER SIX

When he thought about it, which was hardly ever, he didn't consider himself lucky. Too many times, for no apparent reason, events just seemed to go against him. Yet earlier today, one of those rare bits of good fortune had come his way. In fact, as things eventually turned out, it might have happened twice.

After his victory over Bruno, he still had a corner to take back and 200 newspapers to sell. With a canvas bag filled to the top with today's edition, he approached his corner with apprehension. A tall boy with his back to him was already there and busy selling papers. There'd been times when he fought more than once in a day, but fortunately it didn't happen often. He was prepared, but not anxious for the second conflict.

"I believe this is my corner," he announced in his loudest voice.

As the boy turned and saw who it was, he froze where he stood. "Oh no, it's you again," said the same German boy from last year.

Not knowing if the boy had gotten any better as a fighter, he decided to run a bluff. He threw his cap to the ground and began pulling his canvas bag over his head, as if a fight was imminent.

Before the bag reached the ground, the boy had turned and sprinted back up the street without another word.

Then, just like the previous two days, his papers practically sold themselves. *Thanks again, Mr. Dempsey.*

Now it was time to meet up with his friends at the Emporium for a cold bottle of pop. This was a rare treat saved only for Saturdays and only when his tips totaled more than a dollar.

"Any trouble getting your corner back?" Sordi asked.

"Nope. Turns out it was the same German kid from last year" he replied. "Gave it up without a fight. So, how'd you and your mangy dog get here so fast?"

"Bite him, Bodie. Bite him," Sordi commanded his faithful mutt.

"I was only kidding, Bodie," he quickly announced. "So, what piece of good luck got you here before me?"

"You know ol' Michael Purl, the friendly owner of the Copper Crown Cigar Store?" he answered. "He showed up about 7:30 and bought 150 papers. Said his saloon was still packed with an all-night poker game and everyone wanted to read about the big fight."

Both boys knew Prohibition had made it illegal to sell alcohol in America since January. They also knew Montana had been dry for more than a year before that. Since then, most of Butte's more than 50 bars had dropped the term *saloon,* and added "cigar store" to get around the police. Word had it, despite the new law, it was 'business-as-usual' in and around Butte.

"Hey Sordi, you want to come over for supper tonight?"

"Sure. I'll bring some of Poppo's homemade salami," Sordi answered. "I know your father really likes it."

"Be sure to bring Bodie," he added. "You know how much Jessie loves that big mutt."

For the past two years, Guisseppe Luigi Sordino—everyone just called him Sordi—had been one of the two best things about being stuck here in Butte. He was the brother he'd always wanted. The two of them were inseparable in class, after school, selling papers and almost every weekend. Come suppertime, it was likely one was at the other's more-often-than-not. They'd spend hours sharing stories of their childhood before they met and what they planned to do when they were old enough to finally escape Butte. Sordi's dog Bodie was the final member of this close-knit clan they called the "Three Musketeers". Bodie was short for *bodacious*, a word Sordi loved to use to describe the many incredible sights and events that filled his life most every day. He'd learned it in class the week before his father had brought home the stray puppy two years earlier.

Sordi was also different from the other hard-working, struggling-to-survive residents of "the hill." He was openly grateful for what little he had in life. He was almost always happy, and he was funny. Not just a little bit funny. He was wet-your-pants funny. In an instant, he could take you from being very sad or upset to laughing so hard you couldn't breathe. And it always seemed to start with only one phrase in his exaggerated Italian accent, "You nodda, gonna believe…" From there, the tall tale could and would take off in any direction. But you didn't care because he was generally the source of the laughter. Not the story. Sordi was and would always be his very best friend.

A few inches less than five feet, he was noticeably shorter than his peers. However, he was well muscled and unusually strong for his size and age. His father John had been Butte's finest blacksmith for more than twenty years. While each was a bit shorter than most, they were not to be taken lightly.

After some thirty minutes of waiting on the front steps for the rest of their gang, they entered the Emporium with Bodie in tow and purchased a cold pop. With drinks already open and in hand, they joined the line waiting to pay the cashier.

"Boy? Boy?" barked the well-dressed, clearly overweight man as he pushed past the long line and up to the counter. "I'm in a big hurry. Ring up my purchase immediately."

Several of those waiting in line mumbled a bit, but no one made an honest effort to correct the man's rude behavior. Neither he nor

Sordi cared much, paying more attention to their cold sodas and a big display of new lunch pails.

"Excuse me sir, I was here first," came a voice at the head of line. He glanced past the lady in front of him, but couldn't see who was talking.

"Young lady, do you know who I am?" the man replied indignantly.

"Yes sir. You're the rude man trying to push his obviously excessive weight around to get special treatment," the voice replied.

The man turned to the clerk and announced, "Young man, I spend a good deal of money in this store every week. If you do not ignore this little strumpet and take care of me immediately, I'll have you fired."

Skinner and Sordi looked at each in amazement and decided they needed to get a better look at this spirited woman. They gave up their place in line and moved down another aisle to get closer. The female voice grew even louder.

"Sir, if you don't remove your package from this counter this instant, I'll punch your fat belly so hard you won't be able to eat for a week! And we all can see how that would make you very unhappy," boomed the still hidden voice.

"Well, I never," said the man as he turned and stomped out of the store. He left his package on the counter.

Everyone in line cheered and applauded this spunky young girl for standing up to one of Butte's so-called elite.

Skinner worked his way around a stack of 50-pound nail kegs to get an unobstructed view. And there she was.

Looking about his age, she was slightly taller than Sordi, but with a similar muscular build. Her hair was so black it looked almost blue. Cut short, it hung just below her ears; different from most girls he knew. Her face was round like a silver dollar, with a small, slightly pug nose, stuck squarely in the middle. She had large cheekbones, high on her face just like his Indian grandmother. She was wearing a red, long sleeve work shirt, just like the one he wore the day before. Her faded blue overalls and dark, square toe boots looked just like those Sordi had on today. He didn't know if was the way she looked, or the way she spoke to that man, that amazed him the most.

"Hey, let's get back in line so we can get out of here. We got things to do," Sordi yelled.

He didn't respond, because he couldn't. He was paralyzed. He waited for her to look his way, maybe even smile at him. She didn't. Finally, she did look, but it was a mere glance and it paid no more attention to him than the axe handles stacked on the shelf to his right. And then she was gone.

The rest of the day was just a blur, as he tried to figure out what it was about her that made him go a little crazy. Not once since he'd moved to Butte had he ever thought about a girl as anything but a friend or classmate. *Now he wondered how this one could change all that, in just a few minutes?*

CHAPTER SEVEN

Unlike most miners in Butte, especially those over 30 like he was, Sam had managed to survive almost four years without any serious injury. There'd been a couple broken bones in his hands and arms, but nothing that would keep him out of the mines for more than a day or two. However, he had noticed a slight persistent cough these past few months and that really worried him. He'd told no one; especially his family.

"Hey Sam, haven't seen you for a while," yelled the Bell-Diamond's shift boss as he joined the other ten men climbing aboard the express elevator to take the one-thousand-foot ride to the bottom of the shaft. "You lose another partner?"

"Yeah, everyone likes the money, but few are tough enough to last very long," he answered with a smile. "How 'bout you? Wanna make some real money for a change?"

"No thanks. I've seen you work and it ain't pretty," he yelled as the elevator began its rapid drop inside the mountain.

A decent partner was critical to the success of the miners like him. Ambitious and driven, they chose to bid on the tougher, more dangerous jobs, instead of settling for a union job with the same pay, at the same mine, day after day. Then, if all went well, he'd make at least double the average wage in about half the time. The work was harder and more treacherous, but he only cared about making as much money as he could, as fast as possible. Like every member of his family, he hated being stuck in Butte. It was especially tough on him being locked inside a mountain every day, instead of outside in the fresh air like he was on the farm. But he knew what he—they—had to do to change things for the better.

"Hey, O'Brien, keep your filthy hands off our good workers," said a voice at the other end of the elevator platform. "We need them to make our quota."

He ignored the comment, but knew the man was right. He was here in need of a good partner.

"Did ya hear me, ya miserable Irish maggot?" the man persisted.

He remained silent and stared straight ahead as the elevator plunged deep into the dark, narrow shaft that smelled of rotting eggs.

"Take it easy, Moric," said the shift boss. "We don't need any trouble here today. We got plenty of rock to dig for the next ten hours. After that, if you're still feeling frisky, then do what you will."

He went about his work without incident for the rest of the morning. When the meal break whistle sounded at eleven, he grabbed his lunch pail and headed for a dry spot back up by the main shaft.

"Look out O'Brien," came the yell behind him. Instinctively, he dropped his pail, ducked his head, and turned back to see what was happening. He expected a falling rock or beam. Instead, he felt the breeze of a shovel blade swing just past his cheek. It was Moric, and he was ready to do some serious damage.

The massive Hungarian, at more than six feet tall and 250 pounds, tried to retrieve the shovel he had stuck deep in the ground, but Sam quickly kicked the handle out of his hands. Then Moric lunged, reaching for him with his large, calloused hands. He was too slow and missed completely, landing flat on his face in the mud.

Sam stepped away, raised his fists into fighting position and waited. Moric stood, wiped the mud from his coveralls and hurriedly searched for his shovel. When he saw him standing on it, he shook his head, turned, and walked back down the main shaft towards the others who had gathered to watch. Fighting in the mines was not for sport. It was generally serious and often ended in death. It was obvious Moric knew he was overmatched in a fair fight, so he chose survival over pride.

He walked over to the young man whose yell had saved him from the cowardly attack. "Thanks for the warning," he said and offered his hand.

"I sure don't mind two fellas fighting. I just don't cotton to no backstabbin'." The young man stood and shook his hand. "I heard those guys call you O'Brien on the ride down. What's your first name?"

"Sam. What's yours?"

The tall, lanky man replied, "Russell. Russell Green. But friends back home just call me Stretch."

"How old are you Stretch?"

"Be twenty-three on Christmas day this year."

"How long you been a miner?" he asked as they found a dry spot to sit and eat their meal.

"Been in Butte about three weeks," Stretch answered. "Back home in Benham, Kentucky, I worked in the coal mines for more than five years. My daddy worked in them too. He died earlier this year in a cave-in. My momma told me to get out of there or I'd die too. Sure didn't think I'd end up back underground so quickly, but it pays the best, that's for certain."

"Where you staying?" he asked.

"Some dump of a boarding house over on Granite," Stretch answered. "Six guys crammed in a small room with two lousy meals each day. But it's all I can afford for now."

"Young man, I owe you big time for what you did today. It surely saved me from a bad beating. Maybe even saved my life," he said. "Would you come to my home tonight for supper? Won't be a lot, but my wife Kathryn's a damn good cook. Sides, I'd like to talk to you about your future. I believe it's about to change for the better."

CHAPTER EIGHT

The walk from the Bell-Diamond Mine to the O'Brien's tiny L-shaped cottage on Pacific Street took about 20 minutes. When Sam was forced to work without a partner, as he had been for the last two weeks, he chose to stay close to home. The winner of several digging contests over the past four years, he was one of a handful who could work at any mine, any time he chose. He used the walk to lay out his plan for their mutual success.

"Stretch, there are only two ways you can make a really decent living working the mines," he began. "One is join the union and do whatever they tell you. Follow the herd from one mine to another, making five or six dollars a day, six days a week. I call that being a mule."

"Ain't that what most of these fellers do?" Stretch asked.

"Yes. And for them, that's just fine. It beats being a farmhand or wrangler for a dollar a day and room 'n board."

"Not sure I wouldn't rather work on farm for a buck a day. Except with my daddy gone, momma's counting on me to send enough money for her and the children to live on," Stretch lamented. "I can do that if I keep my head down, mind my own business and shovel more ore than the next guy."

"Stretch, I'm here in this hell-hole for just one reason – make enough money as fast as I can to buy back the farm I lost four years ago. Sweetest little peach orchard you ever saw. 40 acres of God's gift to man. A nice home, friendly neighbors, and air so clean and pure you could feel your lungs loving every breath."

"What happened, Sam?" Stretch asked.

"Too long a story for right now. Let's just say I was young and arrogant and ignored the help and warnings of my good neighbors. In less than 24 hours I had lost everything to a killer freeze," he said.

"So, what's the other way to work the mines?" asked Stretch.

"My way. Together, if you're willing to work as hard as I do, we can bid on jobs the mules can't or won't do and we get paid a bonus. Most times we're paid a week's wages for just two or three days' work. We're always makin' at least twice what a mule can earn. Often, it's three or four times more," he said with an eagerness that clearly had Stretch's attention. "Folks around here call it being a bull."

"So, what's the catch? Why doesn't everyone do that?" Stretch asked.

"Lazy. Most folks are just plum lazy," he said as he stopped on the front porch of his cottage. "Besides, they're making a pretty good wage just doing the minimum. They're content with what they have. They've never tasted a warm peach cobbler, made with fresh, juicy Sierra Golds, just picked from the orchard that morning. I have. And will again."

"That's it? That's the only reason all these men settle for making so much less?" asked Stretch. "You said something about the jobs they won't do."

"Won't do them cause they're yellow. Look at Moric. He wouldn't take me on face-to-face. Tried to kill me with my back turned," he said as he drew closer to Stretch's face. "Most of these men are just plain cowards and afraid of doing the tough jobs. I figure you're not like them. Am I right?"

Stretch just stood there staring back into Sam's eyes.

Nothing more was said as the two men entered the house, Stretch forced to duck his head as he entered. Sam introduced him to each member of his family and announced he'd be joining them for supper.

"I've never seen anyone as tall as you," his daughter said and held out her hand for him to shake. "How tall are you?"

"Near as I can tell, 'bout six feet, six inches," Stretch answered.

"Aren't you too tall to work in the mines?" she asked.

"Well, it does cause a few problems now and then," Stretch began. "But if I just bend a little more than most, I can still get the job done when space is a little tight."

"Just after we moved here, Father forgot his lunch pail one morning," his son interrupted. "I took it to the office, but the shift boss took me down into the mine because he didn't know him. It was dark, very hot and the shaft was very small, even for me. I could hardly breathe and I was only down there a few minutes. I don't know how Father does it."

"Mining's not for everyone," Stretch replied with a smile.

"By the way, that's my sister Jessie, and I'm Skinner."

"Howdy, Jessie. Skinner. I got six younger brothers and sisters back home in Kentucky. I been missin' them badly since I left home in April. It's nice to be around a family again," Stretch added, his voice trailing off.

"Welcome to our home young man," Sam's wife said while stirring some stew at the stove. "Now tell me, what does your mother call you? I'll bet it's not Stretch."

"No ma'am, she doesn't. She prefers Russell."

"So do I. Russell it is," she said. "So, Russell, doesn't matter if you're short or tall, friend or family, everyone cleans up before eating at my supper table. You and Sam go out back and wash up. This food is almost ready."

With family conversations normally held until after everyone had finished eating, this meal was filled with everyone asking Stretch an endless stream of questions. At the same time, Sam could only think about how much money he was losing each day without a partner. Even a bad partner, and he'd had plenty of those, allowed him to make at least $10 a day, instead of the $5 or $6 the union jobs were paying. It was time for him to close this deal with Stretch.

"Kathryn, my love, this was another fine meal," he finally announced. "I'd like to speak with young Stretch alone for a bit."

"Thank you, Mrs. O'Brien. Best meal I've had since I left home," Stretch added.

"You're more than welcome, Russell. I hope to see you here again soon," she said as she cleared the plates from the table. "If Sam will give me some warning, I promise there'll be bigger portions next time."

The two men remained at the table alone and he began, "Stretch, I'm running out of time. I need a partner and I need one now. I've already lost more than a hundred dollars these past two weeks without a partner."

"Sam, I'm in," Stretch announced.

"Now, before we shake on this, I need two things. First, I need to remind you one last time, this is damn dangerous work. Maybe not much more than taking a union job in a mine, but some.

"I understand," he replied.

"And, I need you to write down your mother's name and address and give it to my wife, just in case something happens to us."

This time, Stretch paused a moment before answering, "I'll do it tonight before I leave."

The two men stood and shook hands.

"Done. And done," he said.

"Agreed," said Stretch.

Later, Sam laid in bed thinking about his apparent good fortune. With just a few breaks, he, and his family, and maybe Stretch too, could be back on their farm by this time next year. He also knew this rare piece of good luck came none too soon. Strong as he was, he didn't know how much longer his aging body could hold out.

CHAPTER NINE

For Skinner, the past few days had been anything but normal. Sure, he'd still sold all his newspapers twice a day, read a few chapters in his new book and teased his sister at every opportunity. But instead of meeting up with his gang after the morning's sales, he'd gone off by himself on a special mission; a mission to find that amazing girl from the Emporium.

Finally, after four days of searching every store in Butte, he gave up and rejoined his gang at the Daily Post's loading dock after a long Friday afternoon of selling his papers.

"She's just a girl," Sordi said. "They can't play baseball. They can't play football. And they certainly can't fight."

"Didn't you say she threatened to punch that old fat guy at the Emporium?" asked Eddie Slevin, the tallest of Skinner's five-member gang and probably his closest friend after Sordi. He was also the one the girls followed around like little love-sick puppies. The gang had agreed early-on, if there was a dandy amongst them, Eddie and his long black, wavy hair and "pretty-boy" dimples was clearly it.

"Ah, it was just talk," Sordi replied. "She didn't really do it."

"I think she would have," he added quickly. "I don't think she was bluffing."

"So, what are you gonna do if you find her?" asked Bobby Murphy. From another Irish family, he was the largest member of the gang, but his size wasn't his most striking physical characteristic. That label would go to some of the brightest red-orange, long, curly hair in Butte. Had he not been such an unusually large and strong child during his earliest years in Butte, he may not have survived the verbal and physical taunting from the older kids.

"Don't know," Skinner said shaking his head. "Guess I'll just try to talk to her for a while."

The last member of the gang was Jackie Lynch. He was about average height, but extra thin and very flexible, like one of those reeds growing down by the stream. He was also the fastest runner in Butte - bar none. The past two years he had won the annual Fourth of July race from downtown Butte to the top of Mount Spaulding and back, by more than two full minutes. Born in County Meade, Ireland, Jackie was the gang's only full-blooded Irishman. When asked his name, he would often say he was, "The Honorable Jackson Francis Lynch, Himself." Around the gang, he answered to Jackie.

Lynch's family consisted of just one younger brother and his father, who worked as a clerk in a local bank. Just after the family moved to Butte some eight years ago, his mother had received her Montana nursing credentials and taken a job at St. Michael's Hospital as a registered nurse. On the third day of her new job, there was an explosion at the Parrot Mine. Mrs. Lynch, a doctor and four orderlies were helping some of the survivors near the opening of the mine when a second explosion deep in the mine caused the ground under their feet to give way. It took more than a week to find all the bodies. Lynch, a devout Catholic, talked freely about the accident, almost always adding his mother was in heaven and he'd be with her soon enough.

"It would be my honor to meet this fine young lady, Mr. O'Brien. But it would not be so good for you, as she would surely choose me over some skinny Irish, Indian half-breed," Jackie announced with profound confidence.

Within the confines of the gang, almost everything was open to criticism and ridicule. Even the little-known fact that Skinner was Irish on his father's side, and part Cherokee Indian on his mother's side. Had someone outside the gang ever dared call him anything but Irish, blows would have been thrown at once.

Part of the gang's strength came from knowing they could talk about anything when they were together. Eddie was the best at taking a painful topic and making fun of it. Nothing was off limits to his quick wit and strange sense of humor. Not even his own family troubles were protected.

Born in Boston, Eddie's father had been a policeman who was caught taking bribes from Irish gang leaders. Choosing flight over prison, his father brought Eddie's mother and two younger sisters to Butte a little more than six years ago. Like most, his father now worked in the mines and like most, he drank far too much. During their first few years here, Eddie had been forced to defend his mother and sisters from his father on many a late Saturday night. Back then, the young boy suffered serious beatings for his bravery. Now, with Eddie nearing six feet tall with lots of muscles, the fights had stopped, but his father's drinking hadn't. Eddie was clearly the man of the family and took pride in caring for his mother and two younger sisters.

Even with all the turmoil and pain in his life, Eddie seemed to love Butte and all its problems and this truly baffled Skinner, who couldn't wait to get back to California. The two of them would argue for hours, boring the others, and never moving closer to any kind of agreement.

Bobby's family was more traditional Irish, with three sisters and three older brothers. His father and mother owned a small grocery store at the end of Mason Street, nearest Dublin Gulch. They did a good business and were well-liked by the strong Irish contingent that lived nearby. His father's only downfall was his generosity. Bobby had said on many occasions that if his father ever collected on all the IOUs he had in the cash register, they'd be able to move to Crocker Street with all the other wealthy people. And yet, Bobby was clearly his father's son, gladly sharing every nickel and dime he ever had in the pockets of his favorite faded green corduroy pants.

For whatever reason or reasons, be they big or small, he knew this small band of scrappers was more than just a gang of boys looking for a little harmless fun. He didn't know what to call it— fate or just plain old good luck— but he now had four friends he could count on, no matter what. Maybe Eddie's fondness for Butte was slowly beginning to rub off.

"I want to thank you all for your kind and comforting conversation about something you know little or nothing about," Skinner said sarcastically.

"We're only looking out for our pal," Eddie added.

With the small talk over, he tossed his empty canvas bag up on the loading dock and started walking towards the alley and the trip home. After just a couple of steps, he stopped and turned back towards the gang.

"Sordi. They're coming," he yelled.

That was the signal another gang was nearby and a fight was imminent. The boys quickly lined up shoulder-to-shoulder next to Skinner and prepared for the attack.

Seconds later, a gang marched out from behind the three-story, red brick Brammer Shoe building. There were seven of them and each carried a short, black wooden club about two feet long. It was the Clackers from Parrot Flats. They were a tough gang with a reputation for doing serious damage with their handmade weapons.

"We're taking over your corners," yelled the boy leading the pack. "So, get lost punks." He was taller than the other members of his gang, but no taller or bigger than Skinner.

Immediately, Bobby broke ranks and tackled him and another boy on his right. Taking out the leader from opposing gangs was a tactic Skinner had suggested to Bobby from the beginning. He loved it. And he handled it well.

Lynch was the only casualty in the short-lived fight. He'd caught a nasty blow to his right ear that split it wide open and sent him to the ground. Eddie had already dispatched his attacker with a left right combination to the face that sprayed blood everywhere, when he noticed Lynch on the ground. Two large strides with his long legs and he was on top of the smaller kid. One solid, overhand right and the boy landed flat on the ground.

"Let's get out of here," yelled the Clackers' leader. He'd recovered from Bobby's initial assault and clearly wanted no more. Within seconds, the gang had disappeared back around the corner of the building as Skinner surveyed his gang for casualties.

"Lynch, you okay?" he asked.

"Yeah. Thanks to Eddie," he said, holding a handkerchief to his bleeding ear.

"Everyone else, all right?" he asked. He walked over to Lynch and inspected the damaged ear.

"You nodda gonna believe," Sordi started, and the whole gang erupted in laughter before he could even say another word.

"See you guys in the morning," he said, a signal today's events were over.

"You comin' over for supper?" he asked Sordi as they wandered up the alley together.

"Nope. Got my little cousins coming over tonight. See you at the docks."

The two friends went their separate ways and almost instantly Skinner's thoughts returned to the young girl. And so did his frustration. *What was it about this one girl that wouldn't let him think of anything else? The more she consumed his thoughts, the madder he got at himself for being so weak. Sordi was right. She was just a girl. Wasn't she?*

Still fuming after the forty-minute walk up the hill, he shoved open the front door to his home. Before he had taken a second step inside, his sister announced, "Jimmy, meet my new friend, Sarah."

It was her.

CHAPTER TEN

After he finally managed to mumble "hullo", and with his eyes firmly locked on the floor in front of him, he marched straight past his sister and her new friend. At his bed and out of sight of the young girl, he flopped down on the edge and lowered his head between his knees. His was dizzy, his stomach churned with a loud gurgle and he struggled to slow down his rapid breathing.

"Jimmy, are you okay?" his mom asked as she stuck her head around the corner.

"I'll be all right in a minute, mother," he stammered.

"We're having a nice chicken supper tonight to celebrate your father and Russell working together," she continued. "He should be here in a few minutes.

"What? Who? What did you say?" he asked. Then he slowly straightened up, his breathing slowing to a more normal—pre-girl sighting— rate.

"Russell. But it's all right if you call him Stretch," she replied. "You met him a few days ago, here at supper. Today was the end of their first week working together."

Ignoring his mother's last comment, he asked, "Who's the girl? Where she from? How'd Jessie meet her? What..."

"Slow down, Jimmy," his mother said. "She's just a girl Jessie met at Dr. Tom's office today. She brought in a sick puppy."

"So, what's she doing here?" he demanded. "Who told Jessie she could invite her to our home?"

"Jimmy," his mother said firmly.

He knew he had said too much and offered a quick retreat. "Sorry, Mother. Of course, she's welcome. Just like me, Jessie can bring anyone she wants to supper. I'm sorry I said that." He stood, gave his mother a quick hug and headed to the back porch to wash his face and regain his senses.

A few minutes later, Stretch joined the gathering and after a brief introduction to Sarah, they all took their assigned seats. As always, when they had guests for supper, Sam began the conversation with numerous questions. Tonight, he started with their newest guest.

"Well, Sarah, welcome to our home," his fathered offered. "It's not much to look at, but you'll always find a friend and a good meal here."

"Thank you, Mr. O'Brien," she responded in a strong, confident voice.

"Now, tell us a little bit about yourself and your family. What's your last name and why are you here?"

"Grigsby. Our family name is Grigsby," she replied.

"Well, I guess the short version is we're here because we lost our farm in North Dakota to some really bad weather."

"That's the same reason we're here," blurted his sister.

Sarah ignored the outburst and continued, "My father, mother, three brothers and I made the trip from the Red River Valley up near the Canadian border to Butte about a month ago. It took us more than three weeks, travelling 10 to 12 hours a day."

"Why come to Butte?" his father asked.

"Our family wasn't the only family hurt by the two-year drought," she explained. "There was just no farm work to be had in the Valley, unless you were young, single and willin' to work for a dollar a day."

"So, if farming is in your blood, why not head south where farming tobacco is making everyone rich?" his father asked again.

"Daddy don't believe in smoking or drinking, so he and my brothers said no to that right off," Sarah snapped back.

"Okay. So why come to one of the wildest cities in America if he doesn't believe in all that?" his father pressed.

"Newspapers back home been carrying stories about how the copper mines in Butte were making folks rich," Sarah answered. "They said the mines were always looking for hard working men who'd put in long hours for good pay. Daddy said we'd come here for a couple three years and make enough money to go back home and buy some new land. Like I said, farming's in our blood."

"Sound familiar, Sam?" his mother asked.

His father ignored the question and asked, "How long did you say you've been here?"

"About a month," Sarah said. "We left Red River as soon as the snow cleared and we could travel the roads."

"Your father or brothers find any work yet?" His father asked.

"Yes sir. The papers were sure right about finding a job," Sarah stated firmly. "But it seems they were not so right about the good pay. They also forgot to mention how expensive everything is here."

"Like what?" his mother asked.

"Like a place to live," Sarah said. "The five of us are crammed into a very small one-bedroom shack further up the hill in a place called Meaderville. It's all we can afford right now."

"Welcome to Butte," his mother added with a clear note of sarcasm.

He listened intently to the new girl's story. He found himself staring closely at her as she spoke. She wasn't like most girls who almost whispered when they spoke. She was loud, confident, and straight forward. She often used her hands in big sweeping gestures when trying to make a point; just like Sordi. And all the time she spoke, she never once glanced his way. It was time to put her to the test.

"How old are you?" he asked.

"How old are you?" she replied quickly.

"Huh? What? Er, a… I'm 15," he stammered. "So how old are you?"

"Why do you want to know?" she replied, finally turning slowly to face him.

"Don't really care," he said. "I was just wondering if you'll be in Jessie's class this fall."

"I won't be here this fall," she said, ignoring the age question. "I hate it here. The air is always filled with some kind of dark, grey smoke and it just plain stinks. Ain't fit for breathing."

"Butte takes some getting used to, that's for sure," his mother said. "After a few months or so you won't even notice it, until you head up into the high country where the air is so crisp and clean you just drink it in."

"Don't know about that," Sarah replied and then continued her tirade. "But the people—except for you folks and a few others we've met—they're always in a hurry and downright rude. I almost had to punch a big fat man over at the Emporium last week. Darned if he didn't try to push past me when I was standing at the front of the line."

He couldn't help but smile. Out of the corner of her eye she noticed.

"You think that's funny, buster?" she asked with a cold, hard stare.

"Naw. My friend and I were standing in that same line," he replied. "We saw and heard what happened. He deserved what he got."

"Just the same, I'm getting out of here as soon as I can. This place just ain't meant for farming folks to live in," she said.

Before he could catch himself, he asked, "Where will you go?"

She stared at him for a moment, as if seeing him for the first time. The room went silent. Finally, in a little softer tone, she said, "Well, my aunt on my mother's side lives in Boston. She might let me come there, if I decide to ask."

The two of them looked at each other for a few more seconds before Kathryn announced, "Time for dessert. I made a nice apple pie for the occasion."

The big meal his mother had prepared especially for Stretch, his father's new partner, had clearly been overshadowed by the arrival of this strange new girl. *A girl unlike the others, he thought. One who didn't act like a girl. One who didn't dress like a girl. And yet, she was still just a girl. So why was he already trying to figure out how to keep her here in Butte?*

CHAPTER ELEVEN

Today was his fourth Fourth of July celebration since moving to Butte. As with every holiday he'd spent here, he wished it would be his last as a resident.

On a good note, this year's celebration fell on a Sunday. That meant no work and all play for the entire family. He was certain this would be a day to remember.

"Hurry Father. We need to be at the lake before nine," he urged.

"It's only seven. We have plenty of time," his father replied.

"Sordi and his father are probably already catching fish. Please hurry."

Fishing with his father had only happened a few times since moving here. Back on the farm, it was a regular family affair, except during the harvest in August. Asking Sordi and his father, John, to join them on their outing up to Shaver Lake was a welcomed first.

When they returned home a few hours later, Sam carried an old wicker creel full of football shaped rainbow trout. John, a top-notch cook, offered to clean and cook all 15 and bring them to the picnic later that day. The outing had been everything he had hoped for and more. For the first time, John and Sam had spent more than just a few minutes talking about the possibility of farming together in the future. John had access to a new variety of grape from Italy that he said made a red wine like none other. Back in Fowler, situated on the east side of the San Joaquin Valley, vineyards and orchards were plentiful and often grew side by side. The idea seemed to have some merit and each one agreed to talk more soon.

As the Sordinos headed home for their own noontime meal, his mother said, "Make sure you two wash those hands before you take a seat at my lunch table." He and his father obeyed without a single word of protest.

Around five o'clock, he was trying to read Mrs. Camp's book when all he could think about was seeing that Sarah girl again. It had been more than a week since he'd seen her and he still couldn't get her out of his mind. Not that he tried very hard.

Then he heard Sordi's booming voice issue marching orders for anyone interested in getting a good seat. It was way too early and much too hot to leave the relative shelter of their small home. No one moved.

"Hey, Skinner, you better get a move on. We need time to see the Great Waldo's hot air balloon up close." Again, no one budged.

Butte was known throughout Montana for throwing some of the best holidays around. On the 4th of July in 1910, several mine owners opened downtown Butte for free food and drink from nine in the morning until midnight. Cost: $10,000. For the Fourth in 1916, the local Elks Lodge #0240 commissioned the world-famous artist, Edmond Carns to build an enormous elk that straddled the intersection of Broadway and Main streets. It was 62 feet tall and 44 feet long, with 24-foot legs. Cost: $8,000.

This year the featured attraction was Waldo the Great and his magnificent hot air balloon. Skinner and Sordi couldn't wait to get a closer look, now that everyone, including Sarah, had finally arrived.

Loaded down with all kinds of food and drink, they trudged over to Butler Mountain and settled down about half way to the top. By the time they found a place and set up their picnic area, Waldo had already drawn a huge crowd.

"May we go see Waldo?" he asked his mother.

"You haven't had a bite to eat yet," his mother replied, holding up a basket of fried chicken.

"We'll be right back, Mrs. O'Brien," Sordi replied.

"Can we go with them?" his sister asked. She was holding Sarah's hand.

"We're not waiting supper for you. If it's all gone when you get back, too bad," his father offered.

He and Sordi led the way. His sister and Sarah followed close behind. It had only been a week since he had seen Sarah, but he was glad she had come along. He had hoped the strange feelings he had for her would disappear, but it was clear they had only gotten stronger.

"We're too late. The crowd's too big," Sordi announced as they neared the mass of people surrounding Waldo and his inflating balloon.

"Let's go this way," he said as he continued down the hill and around to the left.

"No, we gotta go this way," said Sordi. He grabbed Jessie's hand and pulled her off to the right. Sarah glanced briefly at him before Jessie pulled her to the right.

He started to push his way past a small shack when he sensed something was wrong. He turned to his right and saw a large fist coming at his face. He quickly pulled his head back and the punch just missed. Then someone struck the back of his head from behind. The blow was hard enough to send him to the ground on his knees. Before he could turn around to see who hit him, two hands grabbed his ankles and dragged him around the back of a nearby shack. With all the commotion and people pushing and shoving to get closer to the balloon, no one seemed to care about another fight between two young gangs.

When the dragging stopped, he quickly scrambled to his feet and pushed his back flat against the building. He knew what this was. He just didn't know who it was. A quick glance to each side and it was clear Bruno and his gang had come to fight.

"Knew I'd find you here, O'Brien," Bruno said. "Just didn't think it'd be this easy to get you alone." In his right hand was a thick, gnarly piece of oak wood, more than two feet long.

"Only a coward uses a club in a fist fight," Skinner said.

Bruno laughed, as did the other boys. "A club, a rock, a brick. Hell, I'd use a knife if that's what it takes," Bruno said. "Tonight, I'm finally putting an end to your streak of lucky wins." Then he jabbed Skinner hard in the stomach with the jagged end of his club.

Skinner doubled over in pain, his hands reaching to cover his stomach. His shirt was already moist with blood from the deep cut. A solid punch to the back of his neck sent him sprawling to the ground on all fours. From the other side came a hard kick to his ribs just under his left arm. It hurt, but it was the least of the three blows. He took a deep breath, gathered his resolve, and remained on all fours. He watched and waited for the next attack.

"Kick him again," yelled Bruno. "Kick him in the face."

The boot flew at his head from the right, but he was ready. With a slight movement to the left, he easily avoided the kick as it sailed past his head. He grabbed the boot in his hand as he stood, pushing the boot and the boy's leg above his head. His attacker landed flat on the back of his head. He was out cold.

"Grab him. Grab him," ordered Bruno. This time, he sensed panic in his voice.

From his left came a punch at his head. Too slow and too low; he easily slapped it away from its target with his open left hand. He then delivered a powerful right cross on the boy's left cheek that sent him hard on the ground.

Before he could get his back up against the shack, the remaining two gang members managed to grab his arms and pin them under theirs. Bruno closed in to deliver another blow with his menacing club. As he coiled the club high over his head, he suddenly disappeared. Right in front of Skinner's eyes.

It was Sordi. He'd hit Bruno in a full speed run and taken him to the ground in one swift motion. The club flew more than 20 feet away. Bruno appeared dazed, hurt, and confused.

Skinner felt the grip on his arms loosen, as each boy quickly lost their nerve and ran in opposite directions. He watched as Bruno stood back up and searched for the club. Sordi had it in his right hand, tapping it into his left.

"Gonna try to kick me again?" Skinner taunted as he moved towards Bruno.

"What I'm gonna do is finish this thing once-and-for-all," Bruno shouted. Then he threw a wild roundhouse right that missed badly.

Skinner stepped in and countered with a short, tight, left hook into Bruno's exposed ribs that connected with a loud crack. Bruno yelled and backed up.

Taking a quick moment to steady himself, Bruno came at him with a couple of feeble left jabs that didn't come close.

Again, Sordi countered, this time with a brutal right uppercut that caught Bruno fully on the chin. His head snapped back and he fell to the ground. He was clearly beaten and in obvious pain.

Normally, he would stand back and wait for his opponent to yield. Not this time. He jumped down on Bruno and pushed him flat on his back. Sitting on his stomach, with Bruno making no effort to defend himself, he unleashed a savage right, then a left and then another right. With each blow to Bruno's blood-covered face, the rage from the last four years stuck in Butte, and a hundred fights, boiled closer to the surface.

Finally, desperately trying to stop the attack, Bruno thrust his heavy, useless arms in front of his face.

Skinner smiled and then coiled his right hand back to finish his assault.

"Skinner! Skinner! Stop. Don't do it!" screamed Sordi. "Don't hit him anymore!"

He paused, his fist still coiled and ready to crush an already bleeding and badly broken nose. His teeth clenched, he just sat there staring into Bruno's already swelling eyes, trying to decide what to do.

"Jimmy. Please don't do it. You've won. It's enough," came a calm, firm, female voice.

Skinner glanced up and saw Sarah standing just a few feet away. He noticed she wasn't pleading. She wasn't crying. She wasn't afraid. But he knew she was right.

He uncoiled his right arm and dropped it at his side. He stared deep into Bruno's panicked dark eyes with the rage still pulsing in his throat. He slowly leaned down, almost touching Bruno's blood-soaked face and whispered so only he could hear, "Tell me this is the last time we're gonna do this."

Bruno said nothing.

Assuming he could, but wouldn't, he said, "Make me say it again and you'll be more than just sorry."

Bruno finally managed to cough out, "This is the last time for you and me."

The four of them returned to their picnic area up on the hill without a word to anyone about the fight. There was little more conversation between the kids and soon the festivities were over.

Once back home and in bed, he wondered about his actions tonight. *He had never hit anyone while they were down. He had never fought in a rage, although anger had crept into a few of his last fights. Was he becoming just like the other fighters – no longer able to feel compassion for his opponents? Was he now capable of more than just fighting for a win? He needed to talk to Sordi.*

CHAPTER TWELVE

The next morning after they finished selling their papers, Sordi asked him to walk down to the creek with him. Skinner knew his best friend was not happy with what he had done last night. He worried he may have lost him.

"You can't do that, Skinner," Sordi blurted out as they reached the edge of the creek. "You can't ever hit a kid when he's down. Not even Bruno."

"I know," he replied softly.

Sordi paused for a few more seconds and then continued, "If you do, you're no better than the lot of them. If you do, you're not the person I think you are. If you do..."

"I know it was wrong," he said. "I..."

"If you do," Sordi interrupted. "If you do, I can't be part of the gang. And I can't be your friend."

"I'm sorry, Sordi. I don't know what happened," he replied. "I've never hit anyone like that before. But it was like Bruno and all the other punks like him were the only reason I'm still stuck in Butte. I've never been so mad in all my life. Never."

"Hey, I get mad too," Sordi said. "Hell, we all get mad. But we can't let it take control of us the way it did to you last night," Sordi said. "You've had more than a hundred fights and you've never done that before. Not once."

"You're my best friend in the whole world," he pleaded. "If you asked me to, I'd stop fightin' today. I swear I would. I'm so sorry I did that. I promise it won't ever happen again. Are we still friends?"

Sordi stared blankly and then grabbed Skinner's wrists with his pudgy, powerful hands, "If you ever do that again," he paused for a few seconds, the tension building. Then he smiled and said, "You nodda gonna believe what I'll do to you." They each laughed hard and long and then jumped into the creek with all their clothes on. Before this dreadful event, he didn't think their relationship could get any stronger. It just had.

The very next day on his way to his newspaper corner, he was feeling pretty good about things. Sordi was still his best friend and he'd managed to find the mystery girl from the Emporium. He was wondering when he'd get to see her again when two, heavy-set boys jumped on him from out of nowhere. Each was strong and wildly throwing punches from every direction. Fortunately, they were not well coordinated, their movements telegraphed and predictable. The fight lasted longer than most and he suffered several well-placed blows to his face. Yet with two better-placed blows to the always vulnerable nose, victory was apparently his once again.

"You boys okay?" he asked as usual.

"Ve be fine," replied one of them in a heavy German accent.

"We done here?"

"Javohl, mein Skinner."

He didn't think much about the surprise attack, although it was unusual for him to be caught unready. He was far more concerned with Sarah and when he'd see her again.

The next morning, when he was surprised again in an attack at a different location by two more boys, he thought back to the last time he saw his grandmother. It was almost two years ago, here in Butte and as she promised, the only time she would ever visit this 'evil place.'

"Waya, you seemed troubled," his grandmother said. Waya was a Cherokee name she had given him years before when she came to their home in California. She told him it meant "wolf" and was a badge of courage, reserved for only the strongest warriors. He was only eight at the time, yet she already believed he was special.

During her visit to Butte, he made sure he found some time to speak with her alone. "Grandma, since I've been selling newspapers to help earn money for our farm, I've been in several fights," he replied. "I really don't like to fight. I don't want to hurt them and I sure don't want them to hurt me."

"I have always said you have a good heart, Waya," she offered. "Your good nature will prevent you from doing great harm to others."

"But I have to fight if I'm going to sell lots of papers."

"You also have a strong heart. The heart of a wolf. The heart of a hunter," she continued. "You'll do what you need to, to help your family. And the *Yundi Tsundi* will be with you, as long as you need them."

"What did you say?" he asked.

"The *Yundi Tsundi* are the Cherokee *Little People,"* she said. "They've been a part of our culture forever. They are kind and gentle spirits who mostly help children who are in trouble. You won't ever see them. You'll just hear them in your mind."

"How can these little people help me in a fight?" he asked.

"They're very powerful," she replied strongly. "Do not ever question their ability to help. Only accept it for as long as you have it. Then, when they determine you no longer need them or, are no longer worthy, they'll be gone."

"But..." he started to say he was too old to believe in invisible little people who ran around helping children in trouble.

"Speak no more of this," she replied quickly. "It is a gift to be cherished, not questioned," she added. Her stare deep into his eyes told him this conversation was over.

For the last two years, the *Little People* had helped him often and with them, his confidence grew. Yet even with their help and the many victories, he still hated fighting and would go to great lengths to avoid almost every battle.

The fight today was another tough one and lasted even longer than the one yesterday. With his face still visibly injured from the previous fight, the two punks ignored his body and concentrated on pounding his cheeks, chin, and eyes. In the end, it was his uncommon durability that won the day. His two opponents had given their all, but just couldn't stand up to the endless stream of blows to their face and body.

"You guys okay?" he asked, but with a little more respect than usual.

"Yeah," one of them answered as he slowly sat up and rubbed his bleeding nose. "Sure was a good fight."

"We done here?" he asked.

"Yeah, we're done," answered the other, holding his stomach. "The stories about you are sure right. You're one tough fighter."

Realizing the *Yundi Tsundi* were gone because of his last fight with Bruno, he was now forced to rely on his own senses for the first time in almost two years. That meant his daily travels around town were better planned and more carefully thought out. He avoided long, dark alleyways and anywhere south of Broadway. He wasn't scared, just more cautious. He was rewarded with no more fights for the rest of the week. Yet that reward paled in comparison to the good news from his sister late Saturday afternoon. She told him Sarah would be joining them for supper tonight.

CHAPTER THIRTEEN

He sat on his cot, his back against the wall and Mrs. Camp's prized book in his lap. He'd been in this position for more than an hour without reading a single page. Instead, his mind was filled with thoughts of Sarah, even though he'd only seen her once since the Fourth of July. It was a brief encounter at the Emporium and only polite greetings were exchanged before she hurried off. That was almost a week ago. *Would she say something about the fight? What would she say? Would she even want to talk about it? Would she want to talk to him? He had to talk to her.*

A loud knock at the front door, followed by his mother's greeting broke his trance-like meditation.

"Well, hello, Sarah. It's so nice to have you with us again," his mother said. "Can you join us for supper?"

"Hello, Mrs. O'Brien. Is Jimmy here?" she said, ignoring the invitation.

"I'm sorry. Did you say Jimmy or Jessie?" his mother asked.

"I need to speak with Jimmy first," she replied. Her tone was serious, her voice anything but soft.

The kitchen was only 10 or 12 feet from his cot, so he had heard everything. He stood up and casually walked around the corner as if he hadn't. "Oh, hello," he said.

"May I speak with you for a few minutes?" she asked.

"'bout what?" he asked.

"I'd prefer to have this talk in private," she snapped.

"Sure. C'mon out back." He turned and headed out the door into their small yard.

"Sarah, where are you going?" his sister asked as she walked in through the front door.

"This won't take long Jessie," she announced flatly. "We'll be back in a few minutes."

They walked away from the cottage to the far southeast corner near his mother's vegetable garden. He and his father had painfully placed two very large, mostly flat, granite rocks just inside the back fence to be used for seats. He sat on one, expecting her to take the other. Sarah remained standing directly in front of him, her knees now touching his. He felt very uncomfortable.

"Jimmy, I'm not some silly girl who likes little dolls and frilly dresses. I know I'm a bit plain and heavier than most of the girls. I also prefer being outside, winter or summer," she announced. "But I'm kind, honest and faithful to those I call friend. If you and I are going to be friends, I have to know why you hit that boy when he was down."

Feeling like he was on trial, he fired back defensively, "Who said I wanted to be your friend."

"You did," she snapped. "Every time you've looked at me, or should I say, stared at me. We both know it. And by the way, I like you too."

"I never did any such thing," he protested.

"No? Then why'd you spend a week looking all over Butte for me?" she asked. "Maybe I'm dead wrong, but I'm taking that as a sign we're gonna be more than just casual friends."

He could feel the blood rushing to his face and tried to imagine how red it was. “Okay. So, I think I want to be your friend,” he said. “And yes, maybe more, whatever that means. Now what?”

“Tell me why you hit him,” she demanded.

“I can’t tell you why,” he shot back. “Like I told Sordi, I’ve never done that before. I’ve never even thought of doing that before.”

“Nope. Not good enough,” she said and sat down on the rock next to him. “Jimmy, I need to know what happened.”

“I swear, I don’t know where that part of me came from,” he replied. “I’ll cross the street or walk around the block if it helps me avoid a fight. I hate fighting. But that night I just couldn’t stop. I’m so sorry.”

She stared at him for what seemed an hour, when she finally asked, “Are you ever going do that again?”

“No.”

“Do you promise?”

“Yes. I promise. I promised Sordi too,” he added.

“Okay, let’s go inside and have some supper. I’m starving,” she said. Then she quickly walked towards the cottage.

“Seems you’re always hungry,” he said in whisper she could easily hear.

Inside, the family was just sitting down for the evening meal.

“If that invitation is still open, I’d love to join you folks for supper,” Sarah said, looking at his mother.

“Of course, my dear. It’s only a little chicken and dumplings, but I’m sure there’s plenty,” she answered.

“Well, Sarah, what’s been going on in your world since the Fourth?” his father asked.

“Not much, Mr. O’Brien.” She answered quickly. “My brothers say there’s talk of a strike and that has my parents pretty worried.”

“That’s why I don’t belong to any union,” his father said. “Strike or no strike, there are lots of jobs for men like me and Stretch. Of course, there are some mines that only allow union members to work for them, but for every one of those, there are two more that don't care who you are."

"If there is a strike, can my brothers come work with you?" she asked.

"They can, if they leave the union. You can't have it both ways," he answered. "And, once they leave the union, there's no going back. They don't care for guys like me and are always trying to cause us trouble.'

"Oh," she sighed. "Then I think they'll just stay where they are, for now.

"Probably a good idea until they've been here a few years," he began. "Once they build up a good reputation for working hard and always showing up, then the non-union mine owners will come looking for them with their promises of big money. That's why I switched."

"Thank you, Mr. O'Brien," she said.

"Sarah, you've been here to supper a few times now and I'd like to know a little more about you," his father said, a big smile across his grisly face.

She sat there for a minute or so saying nothing. Then she stood up, smiled, and announced proudly, "My father's father married my mother's mother!"

"Oh, my Lord," gasped his mother.

The room fell dead quiet for a few, awkward moments, until his father started to laugh. Soon he and his sister were laughing as well. Everyone, except his mother.

"Please child, please explain before my wife has a case of the vapors," his father pleaded as he continued to laugh.

"Well, it's actually not that uncommon in North Dakota," she began. "Farms in the northern part of the state are very large. Most have more than 25,000 acres. They need that much land to scrape out a living growing wheat. That means your nearest neighbors might be 10 or 15 miles away. And those neighbors are, more often than not, relatives. There might only be a dozen families within a hundred miles," she continued. "Now, consider the harsh winters and hot dry summers and you begin to see how folks don't always live so long."

"But isn't kind of marrying against God's will?" his mother asked.

"It only sounds bad, Mrs. O'Brien," she quickly replied. "When my grandmother, on my mother's side, passed away some five years ago, the only single man she knew close by was my grandfather, on my father's side. His wife had passed two years earlier. So, they already knew each other, and liked each other, so they got hitched. Two completely, separate families with no blood relation."

For a moment, the room fell silent once again, no one looking at anyone else. Then, his mother began to laugh. And laugh. And laugh. Soon everyone was laughing and holding their sides and wiping away their tears of happiness. It had been years since his family had done anything like that.

CHAPTER FOURTEEN

"I'm not ready for this," Stretch complained.

"Son, I wasn't here a week before I entered my first one," he replied. "I didn't hardly know which end of the sledge to use. Damned if I didn't almost win it."

"I don't know, some of these men been doin' this for years."

"Exactly. Most of these men are half dead. Just don't know it," he said. "Besides, you're a natural. Don't know if I've ever seen a stronger, more natural swing of the big hammer."

"I still don't know," Stretch repeated.

"Look, it only costs us five bucks each to enter. If we win, we'll make a month's wages," he explained. "Don't know about you, but I'm guessing your momma could sure use the extra money."

Stretch thought for just a moment before shouting, "I'm in!"

Like cowboys and their rodeos, and lumberjacks with their log-rolling and sawing contests, miners also competed in contests of skill. The most common was rock drilling, either single jacking or double jacking, using one man or two. Today's contest was for two-man teams only. Each team would drill for 15 minutes into specially imported Vermont red granite, alternating between swinging the sledge and holding and turning the drill bits. Five teams at a time would compete on the huge platform raised exactly six feet off the ground so everyone could see the action

"Looks like another good one today. With all 50 spots filled, the winning team will get $500. Let's dedicate this one to your mother and Katy," he said as they approached the staging area.

"Hey O'Brien, we'll be lookin' for you and that beanpole with you when this thing's over," yelled Moric, the big Hungarian who tried to hurt him in the mine a few days earlier. Standing next to him were three equally large, filthy, bearded men with axe-handle clubs propped on their shoulders.

Stretch stopped dead in his tracks, dropped his sledge and started for the heckler and his pack of thugs. Sam quickly grabbed him and whispered, "Not now son. We've got a contest to win. Then we can have it out with those boys." His grip on Stretch's arm was firm enough to let him know he was serious.

They had drawn lot number 10, the last group of five to compete. He liked the position, preferring to know how deep they had to go to win.

"Don't forget to breathe," Sam instructed his strong, young apprentice. "Many a contestant has passed clean out because they forgot we're more than a mile high. One swing; one breath. No exceptions."

"Who does what and when," Stretch asked.

"You'll swing first for five minutes. Then I'll go six. You'll finish the last four. That's where we'll win it."

The team with the deepest hole so far had drilled 42 ½ inches. Respectable, but nowhere near the legendary Mike Kinsella's world record of 51 1/8th inches.

He didn't tell Stretch that he had never drilled more than 40 inches with his four previous partners. He was strong, but never found a partner who was his match.

"Drillers ready? Go!"

After the last five teams had finished, the judges started measuring each piece of granite. When they reached his and Stretch's hole, the 42 ½ inch mark was still the best. They'd be the 49th team to be measured. Only one more after them.

"For the team of O'Brien and Green," yelled the judge with a long pause to draw out the suspense. "A depth of 44 and ¾ inches."

Stretch let out a long, loud yell, along with more than three hundred crazed spectators.

"Steady son. There's still a damn fine team yet to be measured," he warned his youthful partner.

"For the team of Vizcarra and Cappelluti," again the judge paused for effect. "43 inches even."

Sam jumped in the air with a holler he knew Katy could hear some two miles away. "I knew you could do it, kid. I knew you was stronger than any partner I'd ever had," he yelled above the noise of the crowd. He grabbed his young friend around the waist and hoisted him high in the air.

"Let's go get our winnings," Stretch yelled. "I feel like having a few cold beers."

"Our money will be there after work tomorrow," he replied. "Too much cash to be carrying around today. Besides, we have some business to take care of before we get a taste."

The crowds quickly dispersed towards the many saloons that were poorly disguised as cigar stores. He and Stretch moved along with a group headed for O'Malley's. Stretch was the first to get hit with a club. It was a hard smash across his narrow, muscled shoulders. It did little damage.

"Look out on your right," Stretch yelled. It was just in time for him to catch another club headed for his face. He yanked the club from Moric's hand and used it to block another blow coming straight at him. A sharp jab of the club's blunt end into Moric's face crushed his nose and knocked him flat on his back. The other attacker took one look at his friend and ran.

When he looked back around at Stretch, he had one man face down on ground motionless and the other by the neck begging for a breath of air.

"You okay partner?" he asked.

"Haven't had this much fun since I was a kid back home at a pie eating contest," Stretch answered. A huge smile filled his face as he dropped his gasping attacker to the ground.

Arms draped over each other's shoulder, they marched off towards O'Malley's fine cigar store for a growler or two of his ice cold, frothy beer. As Sam walked, he started to believe things had truly taken a change for the better. It was about time.

CHAPTER FIFTEEN

The night he lost the second fight with Skinner, Bruno vowed he'd see him on the receiving end of a beating worse than his. He didn't know how he'd make that happen, but he swore to every member of his gang he'd get it done before the end of summer. By chance, less than a week later, one of Bruno's gang had been over at the smelter in Anaconda some 15 miles away, and heard of a kid who just might get the job done. A kid the locals called Stubbs.

As the noon train pulled into Anaconda, he jumped from the slow-moving railcar. It continued through the town towards the smelter he could see about a mile away. Looking around to get his bearings, he heard what sounded like a boy yelling for mercy. He scanned the area and decided the cries were coming from a small crowd about fifty yards away. As he ran, he hoped it was the Stubbs kid in action. He wasn't disappointed.

The fight didn't draw too many on-lookers. Maybe a dozen teenaged boys, an old crippled man balancing his hunched-over frame on one crutch and two drunks perched on the edge of the sidewalk. They looked to be resting more than watching.

"I give up. I give up. Please, no more," yelled the boy, his face bleeding badly and pressed firmly into the dirt road.

The larger boy, who was obviously in control, ignored the pleas of the panicked child. Instead, he slowly surveyed his audience, apparently looking for some sign of admiration. Maybe some recognition of his unmatched fighting prowess. But there was none and that only made him madder.

He removed his boot from the back of the boy's neck and said, "Okay kid. You can get up."

As the boy pushed himself back up on all fours, the other boy raised his boot and smashed it down hard on the kid's right hand. The scream only lasted a moment or two before he fell back on the ground. He had passed out from the pain.

"Damn," he blurted out. A boy about his age standing near him turned and looked. He continued, "He always like that?"

"Since he was little," the boy replied. "Well, that's not really true. Stubbs was never little. He was always bigger than the rest of us around his age. And he was always beating us up." He turned towards him, "Who are you?"

"Oh, I'm just running an errand for my boss over in Butte," he replied not saying his name. "Gotta pick up some papers at the smelter. Thought I'd come see what all the yelling was about. You say his name is Stubbs?"

"Yeah, it's because he lost all his fingers in an accident two years ago," the replied. "He was bad before that happened. Now he's just about the meanest sum bitch I've ever seen. He likes to fight. But he really loves makin' his victims suffer before he finishes them off."

"You ever fight him?" he asked the kid.

The boy didn't say anything. He just held up a mangled right hand with three of the fingers almost bent in two.

"Damn," he blurted out again. "Does he fight much?"

"You got lucky today. Especially, for a Monday. Ain't many kids left around here who'll take him on," the kid said. "Hell, ain't many grown men willing to face him either."

"Anyone else looking for a good beating?" yelled the nearly six-foot, heavyset kid with extra-large biceps and forearms that dwarfed the deformed stumps at the end of each arm. No one replied.

Two boys cautiously walked over to the badly injured and still unconscious fighter and slowly dragged him away. The rest of the crowd wandered off, seemingly unimpressed with another one-sided victory. Everyone except this interested observer.

"I heard you were tough. Really tough. I just thought you'd be bigger," he said. He was standing more than a dozen feet away in case a hasty retreat was the next course of action. It was obvious to all he could easily outrun the overweight brawler.

"I'm big enough to whip your ass seven ways from Sunday," Stubbs replied. He took a closer look this new kid's still swollen and bruised face and said with a nasty laugh, "Well hell, looks like someone already beat me to it. Who are you?"

"Name's Bruno Dominici. I live in Butte on the south side," he replied. "And I have no doubt you could. But could you do the same to Skinner O'Brien from Butte?"

"Who the hell is that?"

"He's the toughest kid in Butte," he answered.

"Says who?" Stubbs asked as he moved a little closer.

"Says this face. Says the 100 guys he's whipped over the last two years."

"So, he did that to you?" Stubbs asked.

"Yeah."

"How old is he?"

"I think he's 15," he replied.

"How big is he?"

"About my height, maybe a little shorter and lighter."

"Not interested," Stubbs snapped. He turned and headed up the street towards the smelter saying, "Too small, too easy. Like today, not worth my time."

"I've seen him whip three good-sized kids who hit him with everything they had," he yelled. "Damn guy can't be hurt. He fights smart. He's quicker than most. And he never, ever stops coming at you. Next to you, he's the best I've ever seen."

Stubbs stopped, but didn't turn around. "A hundred fights without a loss? Might be worth my time," Stubbs said as he turned back towards Bruno. "Bring him on."

"Won't be that easy. He never starts a fight. Fact is he tries to walk away from most. And, he surely won't travel to Anaconda for a fight," he continued. "You'll have to come to Butte. And, then you'll need my help to set up the fight."

"What's in it for you?"

"Revenge," he snapped quickly. "And with him out of the picture, my gang will run that town."

"What's in it for me? Why should I waste my time on some would-be punk who thinks he's tough?" Stubbs asked.

"How many see you fight here in Anaconda? Ten? Twenty? Maybe thirty for a big fight?" he asked. "How would you like to fight in front of 200, 300 or more?"

"Maybe," Stubbs replied. "I used to get more when they thought they had a chance," Stubbs replied. "Even when I fight guys 18, 20 and older, nobody ever lasts very long. Hell, I killed me a full-grown miner back in March."

"How come you didn't go to prison?" he asked.

"Judge ruled it self-defense. Seems a few days earlier I'd beat up his younger brother pretty bad, so he came looking for me with a knife," Stubbs said. Then he smiled. "Should've brought a gun."

"How about I buy you a soda and we can talk about you coming to Butte?" he asked as he tentatively moved in closer.

The boys walked across the street to a small store where Bruno bought two large colas. Then they came out and sat on the edge of the wooden sidewalk.

"Mind if I ask how your hands got that way?" Bruno asked.

"You mean these?" Stubbs asked as he proudly displayed what was left of his two hands. Each had four jagged stubs just above the first knuckle. Yet, each also had a completely intact thumb. The ends of the four fingers were scarred and covered with a thick gray/black callous. Their coloring made them look dead. And deadly.

"Did it hurt when it happened?" he asked. "Do they hurt now?"

"I never felt a thing—not then; not now. Doc says I lost all the nerve endings," Stubbs answered. "Happened two years ago this month. I was helping my father cut timber up on the Pioneer Range. He was a lumberjack for the Anaconda mine."

"Most lumberjacks are French. Are you?" he interrupted.

"Father was. Mother still is. My given name's Mason Napeel Gillette, but I ain't no frog eater. They're too weak for me. Most of them around here ain't got no backbone. Won't stand up for what they want. Let everyone run over them. Won't say shit with a mouth full." Stubbs finally stopped himself and took a big drink of his cola.

"Sorry. Didn't mean to piss you off," he said quickly. "What happened?"

"We were cutting some big trees on the north slope, really steep. Most 'jacks wouldn't go there. But my dad knew we could make some really good money if we could bring down a few of those big pines. We'd already cut seven trees that morning and the four men running the steam engine up on top were falling behind. Seems two of the trees were too damn big for the chains. They tried to string two chains together, but they finally broke and both trees came rolling down the mountain."

"What did you do?" he asked impatiently.

"I didn't do nothing. I was still chopping as fast as I could; never heard a thing. My father saw them. Dumb, son-of-a-bitch pushed me down the hill instead of saving his own life. First log hit him in the chest and cut his head clean off. Second one hit the tree I was cutting and split it in two. Half fell one way and the other half landed on my hands."

"Well, hell. He saved your life. Why you so mad at him?" he asked.

"I didn't ask him to do it. I wouldn't have done it for him," he said. "Take care of number one. No one else will."

"How long did it take for them to heal?"

"It was about six months before I realized what the good Lord had done for me," Stubbs replied, and then he smiled. "Instead of killing me, he gave me two weapons like none other. I've heard it said that getting hit with these is like getting hit with a hammer. There ain't no give in my little friends," he said. He held them up in front of himself for Bruno to admire.

"Damn," he finally managed to say. "You just might be the one to stop this kid."

"Ain't no man alive who can beat me with just his fists," Stubbs proclaimed.

The two sat and talked a while longer as he laid out how things would go in a few days. Stubbs listened, but he knew he wasn't really interested or even remotely concerned with the details. The fact he was going to fight Skinner brought a smile to his face that lasted for days.

CHAPTER SIXTEEN

Winning last Sunday's contest was the first real fun Sam had had in months. Stretch said the same. It was also a good thing for their partnership. While most mine owners in Butte already knew he was good, the competition clearly showed his partner's equally impressive skill. In the days that followed their win, he decided to take advantage of the temporary fame and publicity. He outbid a four-man crew for a big job at the appropriately named Desperation Mine.

"Sam, you know I trust you. I believe in you," Stretch began. "But taking on a four-man job is crazy. And way out at the Desperation? I've heard it's damn dangerous."

"If I add the money from this one job to our winnings from the contest, I'm less than five hundred dollars short of my goal," he said. "Do you know what it would mean to my family to finally get out of Butte before another miserable winter?"

"Is it worth dying for?" Stretch asked.

"We ain't gonna die. Things are changing. My luck's finally changing. For the first time in my life, I'm catching a break," he shouted. "Now, are you with me, son? Will you help me and my family get back home to our farm?"

He held out his hand and after a few seconds, Stretch grabbed it and shook it hard.

For the first two days, everything went just fine. It was tough work, but other than the steep incline of the mine shaft they were working, it was nothing he hadn't done before. Of course, the incline was what made this a big money job. He and the other old timers knew it was never good to run a spur on more than a six or seven-degree downgrade. Too much weight in the ore cart to move up the hill. This one was a full nine degrees.

"We've been working this shaft for two days, and I'll be damned if I know what we're doin' here," Stretch said.

"This mine has been on hard times for the past couple of years," he replied. "Now when they finally hit a big vein of high grade ore, the darn thing heads off on a bad slant."

"So why don't they just do what the other mines do: dig deeper and start a new horizontal shaft."

"Owners don't have enough money. Nor the time," he said.

"What do you mean?" Stretch asked.

"The mine's owner is a gambler named Brunson. Story goes, he won the mine in a card game five years ago when he was on a big winning streak," he said. "Now he's losing and if he doesn't pay back a gambling debt to a guy named Ivy before the end of month, he loses the mine. And just when she starts to make him some real money."

"So, what makes you think he'll pay us?" Stretch asked.

"Already has," he said. "It was part of the bid. He put our money in a special account over at First Western Trust. All we need to do is find the vein again in the next seven days. If we do, we get paid and Brunson can borrow all the money he needs to keep the Desperation up and running."

"As I said, it's been two days and I ain't seen no sign of copper," Stretch replied. "We ain't going to get a dime for all this work."

"It's there. I know it is," he replied. "It just has to be."

"Hey partner, it's almost time for lunch," Stretch said, "Let's finish this cart and call for the engine. I'm starving."

Against his better judgment, he was breaking one of his basic rules of mining — safety first. To save time, they had remained at the bottom of the shaft each day to eat a quick lunch. The climb back up to the main shaft was more than 100 feet and not worth the time or energy. He took the whistle hanging around his neck and blew two long bursts – the call for the electric engine to come retrieve the rock.

The driver and his helper finally arrived and hooked on to another cart loaded with worthless slag. As they continued to go deeper, it took the old electric engine longer and longer to make the round trip to the elevator. With the extra time, Stretch had piled this one almost to the ceiling. The tunnel was small and only slightly bigger than the train running on the narrow tracks. They each worked all day bent over at the waist.

"See you boys after lunch," said the driver. As the engine began to pull the cart slowly and silently up the steep incline, the helper jumped on top of slag.

"Partner, what if I was to give you my half of the contest winnings, plus the money from this job?" Stretch asked. "Do you think you'd have a job for me back on your farm in California?"

Sam just sat there, unable to speak. In an instant, his mind raced ahead and all that it would mean to him and his family if that happened. Then he returned to reality.

"Son, Katy and I've thought about you comin' with us since the day you saved me from that coward Malik. Nothing would make us happier," he said. "But we don't take no charity."

"All right. How about I buy into your farm?"

"Don't really want a partner," he said.

"Okay. How about we have the bank draw up a document that says you're borrowing the money now and will pay me back over the next couple of years? Plus interest!"

He thought about getting out of Butte this summer and what he'd be willing to do to make that happen. Just as he was about to say yes, he heard the big steam whistle basting from up near the main shaft.

"Runaway! Runaway! Runaway!" came the shouts from above.

A quick glance at each other and they leaped to their feet.

"We need to build us a rock wall on the tracks," he yelled. Without another word, Stretch grabbed his shovel and started digging.

Frantically they worked trying to cover the tracks far enough up the incline to stop the run away from crushing them into the end of the shaft. But the digging was tough and the rocks were too small to stop anything. And the sound of the thousand-pound cart rumbling down toward them grew louder with every passing second.

"Keep digging, partner," Stretch yelled as he turned and started running up the incline.

"Stretch. Stop. Don't do it. Don't go up there," he screamed. He started to follow his partner, but he knew it was useless.

Stretch never looked back and quickly disappeared into the dim light further up the tunnel.

A few seconds later he heard the loud noise of the rumbling ore cart go silent. Sam dropped his pick and fell to his knees.

CHAPTER SEVENTEEN

Russell Green was not Irish. Worse yet, he had said he thought his bloodlines were English. Most Irish living and working in Butte still hated the English for what they had done to them and their country over the past 800 years, especially during the potato famine in the mid-1800s. Yet today, that detail meant nothing to Sam. Russell had first become his partner, and then a trusted friend. As such, he deserved a full service, Irish burial, including a wake.

"Attention everyone," Sam shouted as the crowd from the church approached the entrance to their small home.

"As my grandfather always said, there can be very little mourning for a good man over a cup of tea or a glass of milk. And Stretch was a very good man. So please, help yourself to the more traditional beverages inside and to hell with Prohibition."

He knew the Irish miners considered it disrespectful to allow the remains of a friend—Irish or not—to make the trip to the cemetery without at least one evening with convivial friends. When the death was violent from fire, cave-ins or such, the coffin remained closed but nearby in the home of a friend or relative. Russell's casket was closed, but replaced the O'Brien's supper table for the evening's event.

"Ladies, please join me in the back yard for more civilized conversation," his wife announced after everyone had secured the drink of their choice. Earlier, since this was her first Irish wake, Sam had explained to her that men and women never mingled at a wake. He asked her to take the women outside as quickly as possible.

Then, as the men gathered near the coffin, he noticed a tal, dark skinned man stagger in the front door. He guessed he was just looking for another free drink.

"Don't believe I know you, sir," he said. He offered the man his hand.

"Bet you know this," yelled the man as he swung a small pickaxe at his head.

He dropped his tankard of ale and easily blocked the man's attack. He was clearly drunk and not a real threat to anyone, except himself. Two men standing on either side of the man grabbed his arms and held him in place. His knees buckled, but the men kept him standing upright.

"Whoa, stranger. What's your beef with me?" he asked.

"You bastard. Moric's my cousin," the man said.

"Did you say Moric?" he asked.

"You and your dead partner damn near killed him," he said. The man's words sprayed the remnants of his last whiskey. "I believe it's time you joined that skinny sum bitch in hell!"

"Boys, please escort our friend outside and let Sheriff Johansen take him to the pokey." He laughed it off in front of everyone, but inside it was another painful reminder of how much he hated being stuck here in Butte. And how much he felt this death was his fault.

The men soon turned their conversation back to Stretch's heroic deed. Throwing his body in front of cart to save his partner would surely be remembered and retold for years to come amongst Butte's rough and rugged miners. It would also become another part of his family's tragic saga that started the day they arrived some four years earlier.

The last of the mourners had finally left and as they sat on their front porch, orange and pink light began to fill the skies above.

"This was a proper good-bye, for a damn fine young man," his wife announced.

"He was such a good man. Why did this happen?" he said without any hope of an answer.

"What's happening with the investigation at the mine?" she asked, ignoring the question she knew had no answer.

"Same as always, they protect the owner," he said, shaking his head. "It's being ruled our fault for overloading the cart. Brunson says he's being a good guy and paying the standard $200 for an accidental death."

"Can you fight it?" she asked.

"No use," he snapped. Then, he turned and took her hands in his and said, "I'm sorry, my love. I just feel so damn bad for getting him into this. He was so young and had such a free-and-easy way about him. In just those few weeks, I came to love him like a brother."

"Sam, he knew what he was getting into," she said. "His father was a miner and so was he. It could have happened anywhere, anytime, especially here in Butte."

"I know you're right," he sighed. "But I'd like to do something else for his family, if you agree."

"What is it?"

"I'd like to give them my half of the winnings from the drilling contest," he answered. "It's only $250 dollars, but he sure as hell earned it."

"I think that's a wonderful idea," she answered quickly.

"I also believe he'll be the last partner I'll ever have."

"The last? What do you mean, Sam?" his wife asked.

"I can't do this anymore," he said.

"Can't do what?"

"I can't keep up," he said, afraid to look at his wife. "Stretch was working circles around me every day. He never said a word, but we both knew he was doing most of the work."

"My love, Russell was special. He was young, very strong and so determined. Just like you were 15 years ago," his wife said as she grabbed his arm and squeezed tightly. "You only need to hang on a little longer. Find another partner or two and go hard for one more year and we'll have enough for our farm."

"Don't know if I'll make it another year."

"Yes, you will," she said. "You'll make it for Jimmy and Jessie. You'll make it for me. You'll make it for you."

"I'm tired of going hard," he said. "I'm tired of just surviving. I don't have that many more years, my love."

"You're not that old, Sam," she replied and smiled.

He waited for a few seconds before he turned and looked deep into her eyes and said, "Dammit, Kathryn, I've got the cough."

CHAPTER EIGHTEEN

The train rolled into Anaconda right on schedule. Bruno jumped down and hurried up the street to the Branchwater Saloon; he remembered it was Stubb's favorite hangout. He was worried that it had been more than two weeks since he'd talked the massive fighter into doing what he couldn't: beat Skinner. He hoped he hadn't changed his mind.

"Where the hell you been?" Stubbs asked.

"I'd have been back sooner, except there was an accident at the Desperation Mine," he answered. "Skinner's old man almost died. His partner was killed. There was a big funeral, so I just laid low for a while."

"You still want me to wup that puny little Irish kid?" Stubbs asked.

"I want you to beat him so badly, his mother won't recognize him," he replied. "Then I want you to beat him some more."

"Yeah. Sure. Hey, you wanna go have some fun?" Stubbs asked. "I can fight this punk anytime."

"You better take this kid seriously," he said. "You might be better than him, but you ain't gonna wup him without one hell of a fight."

Stubbs scratched his head and yawned. He asked again, "How about we go throw some rocks?"

Upset at this apparent fool's attitude, he snapped, "Throw rocks at what?"

"Critters," Stubbs replied and smiled. "Stray dogs and cats. Or whatever else wanders through the draw outside of town."

"I'm not much into killing dumb animals," he said.

"Oh, we don't usually kill them. It's just some harmless fun," Stubbs said. He turned back towards his small gang and they all laughed.

"Naw. I gotta get back to Butte on the next train," he said and pulled up a chair. "Besides, we need to talk about a plan."

"What you got in mind?" Stubbs asked.

"His best friend's a little wop they call Sordi. They do everything together," he began. "Sordi's got a big mutt of a dog. They take the damn thing everywhere. So, if I grab the dog, they'll come looking for it. Then I take out the wop and you pound Skinner."

"If they always take the dog with them, how you gonna get it?" Stubbs asked.

"I heard they don't take it fishing," he replied. "Seems the damn dog keeps jumping in the lake. Scares all the fish."

"When you gonna do this thing?"

"Tomorrow's Sunday. They like to go fishing when they don't have papers to sell," he explained. "While they're gone, I'll grab the dog. Then, when they come home and he's not there waiting, they'll come looking."

"Okay. I'll take the noon supply train over to Butte. You meet me there at one o'clock," Stubbs instructed. "If you got the dog, I'll get off. You don't, I'm comin' back to Anaconda and then he'll have to come find me."

The next day the train arrived a little past one o'clock. Stubbs appeared surprised to see Bruno, five other kids and a big mutt of a dog tied with a piece of old rope.

"Well, I'll be," Stubbs said. "Have any trouble getting this big lump of fur?"

"Hell no," Bruno answered. "All it took was a couple pieces of bologna and he was ours. Damn thing's so friendly I just might keep him for myself."

"Dumb dogs," Stubbs said. "They're like rats. All they care about is eating, sleeping and shittin'."

"We'll go down by the Silver Bow," he said. "There's a big clearing hidden by large mounds of tailings. No one'll see us."

"Send one of your boys to get me a growler of beer and a couple sandwiches," Stubbs instructed. "I don't like waiting or fightin' on an empty stomach."

Around five o'clock, one of Bruno's gang came running. He'd been stationed near Sordi's house to help direct the two kids down to the Bow.

"Boy is he pissed," yelled the kid. "And he's right behind me."

"Skinner?" he asked hopefully.

"Naw, just the little Italian kid," the boy replied. "Yelled something about Skinner had already gone home. Said he was the only one coming for his dog."

"Damn. Damn. Damn," he yelled. "I don't give a hoot about the little wop. I want Skinner!"

"We take care of one and the other will be here soon enough," Stubbs assured him. "If I need to, I'll spend the night and whip Skinner in the morning. Then I'll catch the noon train back home in time for lunch."

"You want me to whip the Italian?" he asked.

"Naw. I got plans for the little fella," Stubbs replied. "And his stupid mutt, too."

Sordi appeared at the top of a tailings mound, stopping to scan the area. Several kids were scattered around the opening and on the far side, two larger boys stood next to Bodie.

"That's my dog," yelled Sordi.

"Who says it's your dog?" Stubbs asked.

"Guisseppe Luigi Sordino."

"Pretty big name for such a little wop," Stubbs said.

"Who the hell are you?" Sordi asked.

"The boys call me Stubbs. But you can call me master."

"Did you say bastard? I can call you bastard?" Sordi taunted.

"Oh, you shouldn't have said that," Stubbs replied. "Now I'm gonna have to kill your stupid little dog." He grinned, took a step back and then kicked the dog into the air. It landed hard on its head and front legs almost ten feet away. It made no sound or movement.

Sordi tore off running down the mound screaming and hit Stubbs just above his knees. They flew several feet with Stubbs landing flat on the ground and Sordi on top. Before Stubbs could recover, Sordi jumped on his stomach and delivered a solid left cross that caught him on his cheek and eye. He followed it with a right cross to Stubbs' left eye, splitting the eyebrow, and filling the socket with blood. He stood back up and waited for Stubbs to do the same.

"Not bad for a little runt," Stubbs said. He struggled to his feet and wiped his face with a blue handkerchief from his back pocket. "Can't remember the last time anyone knocked me to the ground."

"It'll be easier this time," Sordi replied. "You're going right back down."

They circled around to the left for a few seconds before Sordi, who was at least a foot shorter and more than 100 pounds lighter, threw a straight left jab into Stubbs' huge belly. He followed it with a hard right and then another left in rapid succession. Stubbs just stood there. Then he laughed.

"My turn punk," he said. He caught Sordi with a single punch on his cheek bone. The sound was so loud they heard the loud cracking noise from 15 feet away. Sordi's eyes were open, but he was out cold on his feet. He stood for a couple of seconds before falling face-first on the ground. The fight was over.

"Jesus Stubbs, you've killed him," he shouted.

"Naw. Just hurt him a little," Stubbs said. "Now comes the good stuff."

Stubbs walked over to Sordi and used his foot to turn the limp body over on its back. Then he maneuvered the right arm away from his side. He raised his large, black boot and then stomped down on the small hand and its short, fat fingers. Sordi moaned, but did not wake up. Stubbs walked around to other side and repeated the attack on the other hand. Once again, it drew a moan, but nothing more.

"Okay. Okay. That's enough," Bruno yelled. Then he moved towards Stubbs, waving his hands out in front of him. "He's had enough. We don't want him dead."

"Sure. Sure. I'm done," Stubbs said. He took a step away and then turned and smashed the half-worn heel of his square-toed boot into the middle of Sordi's ribs. This time, there wasn't a sound or any movement from the mangled body. Stubbs smiled and slowly walked over to the shade of a small tree. He lowered himself to the ground with his back against a large boulder. He grabbed a growler of beer and took a long drink.

He ran over to Sordi, praying he wasn't dead. He leaned down and listened for a few seconds before announcing, "He's still alive."

"Too bad," said Stubbs. "How about the mutt?"

"Looks dead to me," he said as he glanced over at the motionless dog.

"Thought so," Stubbs replied. He grinned some more, then picked up his half-eaten sandwich and stuffed it in his mouth.

"Doc, Cecil. Get over here, quick," he yelled.

Doc Emmert and Cecil Moore were two longtime members of Bruno's gang. He trusted them as much as anyone.

"You gotta get this kid back to town where someone can find him and get him fixed up," he instructed. "Take him over to the newspaper. His friends will be there first thing in the mornin'."

"What about the dog?" Doc asked.

"Take it with you and leave it next to the kid," he said.

"What about that Skinner kid?" Stubbs asked.

"Not now. This whole thing has turned to shit," he answered. "Pretty sure you killed the dog and maybe killed the wop. All hell's gonna break loose."

"I got no worries," Stubbs said. "The kid came at me first. Self-defense. Then he laughed aloud as he started to walk back towards town.

"I don't care. I'm getting' out of town for now," he said. "We'll do Skinner after things quiet down."

"Hell, I knew from the first time I laid eyes on you," Stubbs started. "You're just a miserable coward. No wonder the Skinner kid whipped your ass."

"I'm a survivor," he answered. "If that means going to Denver to live with my cousin for a few months, so be it. But this thing isn't over yet."

CHAPTER NINETEEN

Skinner sat up and swung his legs over the side of his cot. It was earlier than usual, but already a faint light flickered in the kitchen. His mother was making the simple breakfast they ate on workdays.

"Toast and milk are on the table. If you want some oats, it'll be a few minutes more," his mother said. "How come you're up so early?"

"Don't rightly know," he answered. "Something just told me it was time to get a moving." He gulped down the milk, grabbed two pieces of toast, and headed for the front door. "No time for oats."

"Maybe grandma's *Little People* are back and trying to tell you something," his mother added.

"I'm in no danger," he replied.

Before he had taken two steps, there was a loud knock. He opened the door and found Sordi's father.

"Is Guisseppe here?" Mr. Sordino asked.

"No. I haven't seen him since we got home from fishing yesterday," he said.

"He no come home last night," Mr. Sordino said. "His mother and I were hoping he was with you."

"Not sure what he's up to, but he'll be down at the dock this morning" he replied. "I'll head on down and make sure everything's okay. We'll come by your shop after we finish the morning edition."

Heading down to the newspaper at a steady run, his concern began to overtake his optimism. It wasn't like Sordi to do this kind of a thing.

As he approached the newspaper in the dim light of predawn, he didn't see any sign of Sordi or anyone else. He slowed to a walk and moved closer to the loading dock. Finally, his eyes adjusted to the darkness and he spotted a body propped up against the wall, sitting in a pool of blood with the head slumped over on its chest. It was his best friend, with his dog laying across his legs.

"Sordi. Sordi." He ran and dropped to his knees. Gently he lifted his friend's mangled, blood-stained face, searching for any signs of life. There were none. He yelled louder, "Sordi. Sordi. Talk to me."

His eyes swollen shut and covered in dried blood, Sordi parted his lips slightly. Then he licked them and tried to speak.

"He killed my dog. He killed Bodie."

"Who killed Bodie?" he asked.

"Stubbs."

"What? Who?" he asked again.

"Stubbs," Sordi repeated. Then his head slumped back down on his chest. He was still breathing, but the breaths were shallow and rapid.

He didn't know who or what he meant. He didn't care. He had to decide: either leave his friend here and run to get help, or risk injuring his friend even more and carry him the seven blocks up the hill to St. Patrick's Hospital. Without hesitation, he moved Bodie off to the side, then slid his arms beneath Sordi's legs and behind his back and started to run.

Halfway there, he knew they were both in trouble. His arms and legs screamed in agony and his lungs begged for more oxygen. Then, when he stopped for just a moment to catch his breath, he felt Sordi go limp, no longer fighting to breathe.

"Don't you die on me, dammit," he screamed. "Don't you dare leave me here alone." He started running again.

Less than a block from the hospital, he spotted an orderly climbing the stairs to the entrance. With his last bit of strength, he screamed, "Help. Help." Then he dropped to his knees.

"I'm coming. I'm coming," replied the young black man.

In one swift, smooth motion the orderly reached down and snatched Sordi from his sweat-drenched body. In a burst of speed, he was up the stairs and inside.

By the time he caught his breath and reached the lobby, Sordi was nowhere in sight. Still gasping for air, he headed over to the nurses' station and asked a large, heavy-set woman with short gray hair and a scowl on her face if she knew where they had taken him.

"The boy is in the emergency room with Dr. Nelson," she snapped. "You'll need to have a seat over against the wall if you want to wait."

"I don't want to wait, I want to see him. Now," he demanded.

"You can't see him now," she replied firmly. "Now, either go sit down or leave this building."

"You don't understand. He's my best friend. I need to be with him," he pleaded.

"Young man, it wouldn't matter if he was your brother," she said. "You can't go in there."

"But..."

"Sit," she interrupted. "I don't have time to babysit all you young punks who think it's so manly to beat each other up. It's just a waste of the doctor's time. And mine, too."

He ignored the nurse's comments and hostile attitude. He was trying to understand what had happened to Sordi. Strangely, thoughts of Sarah flashed into his mind for a few moments. He wished she were here. Then he realized he had to get word to Mr. Sordino. Once again, he was forced to make a tough choice: stay with his friend or leave him to tell his father what had happened. He jumped to his feet and ran out the door.

As he approached the small wooden building on the eastern edge of town, about a mile from the hospital, he began yelling, "Mr. Sordino. Mr. Sordino. Come quickly. He's been badly hurt. He's at St. Patrick's."

Sordi's father dropped his hammer and yelled to the man standing near him, "Pasquale, run tell Mrs. Sordino they found him. Bring her to the hospital as fast as you can." Then he sprinted off, disappearing around the corner.

His mother worked in the laundry next door. If she hadn't already heard, he needed to find her and tell her.

"Hello, James," said the laundry manager as he pushed open the large swinging doors. "You looking for your mom?"

"Yes ma'am. It's very important," he said.

"Katy. Katy. It's your young, handsome son. Says it's important."

She came running. "What is it, Jimmy?"

"It's Sordi. He's been hurt. Bad. Really bad."

"Where is he?"

"St. Pat's."

She pushed past him in a dead run.

He followed closely behind her as she ran across a walkway between the laundry and the back of the hospital. They entered through a double door on the east side marked "Staff Only."

"Wait here," his mother said. She eased open one of the emergency room doors and disappeared inside.

After a few minutes, she returned.

"How is he?" he asked.

"He's alive," she said. She reached for him to hold him, but he jumped back.

"What's that mean?" he demanded. "What are you saying?"

"Jimmy, he's hurt really bad," she whispered. "Looks like they beat him with a club."

"No. No. No," he cried. "But he's going to live, isn't he? He's going to be okay, isn't he? He isn't going…" He reached out and grabbed his mother, squeezing her hard.

They embraced and stood silently just outside the back door to the emergency room. Then, after several minutes, the silence was interrupted by a woman screaming, "Guiseppe. Guiseppe. My baby. My baby boy!"

CHAPTER TWENTY

They sat huddled together in the small waiting area. Between the sobs and occasional moans, he watched as Mr. Sordino tried in vain to comfort Sordi's mother. It had been almost five hours since the attendants rushed Sordi into the emergency room. His mother had tried to assure the Sordinos that Dr. Nelson was one of finest doctors in the county.

Then the emergency room door pushed open and the doctor came straight over to our gathering.

"He's stable and resting, for now," Doctor Nelson reported.

"Can we see him, doctor?" Mr. Sordino asked.

"As soon as we get him moved to a private room across the hallway from my office," the doctor replied.

Just then the doors swung open and a gurney carrying Sordi moved quickly down the hall.

"Guisseppe. My little Guisseppe," Mrs. Sordino cried out.

Sordi's head was wrapped in so many white bandages. He could only see his eyes, nose, and mouth. He was motionless.

"Before I let you go in to see your son, let me try to explain what's happening to his body," the doctor began.

"I don't care what's wrong with him," Mrs. Sordino screamed. "I just want to hold my baby boy." She stood up straight and started to follow the gurney.

"Please, Mrs. Sordino, let me finish." Doctor Nelson reached out and took one of her hands in his. She stopped and stared up at the tall, thin man.

"You talk," she instructed.

"Your son has some very serious injuries. Someone crushed the fingers on each hand. Then they broke his jaw and shattered the ribs on his right side. Several rib pieces punctured his lungs and he's having trouble breathing. And he's lost a great deal of blood."

"So, what are you doing to help him?" she pleaded.

"We stitched his cuts and set his broken fingers. But he really needs an operation to stop the bleeding and repair his lungs," the doctor answered.

"So why aren't you operating on him now?" questioned Mr. Sordino.

"He's far too weak. We need to give him a blood transfusion and let him recover from the trauma," the doctor replied. "We'll operate as soon as his blood pressure comes up, but no later than first thing tomorrow morning."

"Morning? Morning? He won't be alive in the morning," cried Mrs. Sordino.

"We'll have a nurse with him every minute until we take him in," the doctor explained. "I won't leave the hospital tonight, so I can operate the minute gets stronger."

Holding hands and saying nothing more, the Sordinos shuffled back down the hall and into Sordi's room.

"Doctor Nelson, what can we do now?" Skinner asked.

"You can pray for a miracle, young man."

Then the doctor turned to his mother and said, “Kathryn, I know you’re not a licensed nurse in Montana, but I’d like for you to stay with him for now. I just don’t have enough staff to monitor his condition for the next 24 hours.”

“Of course, doctor,” she replied. “I’m here as long as he needs me.”

“Great. Let me know if there’s anything you need.”

“Would you please let the laundry know where I am?” she asked. “We ran off this morning without saying anything to anyone.”

“Yes. And I’ll make sure the hospital pays you for your time over here.”

“I don’t care about any pay, Doctor Nelson,” she replied. “This boy’s like a member of our family. I’ll stay as long as he needs me.”

“May I go in and see him?” Skinner asked.

“I guess it’ll be okay. But just for a moment,” the doctor cautioned. “He’s not conscious, and he won’t hear you.”

“He’s got to hear me,” he said. “He needs to know I’m here. He needs to know I’ll take care of him.”

As he moved inside, he saw the Sordinos standing on either side of the bed whispering something to their son. He noticed the white bandages around Sordi’s head had started to turn pink. He guessed it was the blood still oozing from his many wounds.

As he inched closer, Mr. Sordino looked up and motioned for him to take his place on the near side of the bed. Then he walked around and joined his wife on the other side.

“Sordi. Sordi. It’s Skinner,” he whispered. “I’m here, partner. I’m right here. I won’t let anything happen to you.” He used the back of his hand to wipe at the tears rolling down his cheeks. As he surveyed the damage some miserable bastard had done to his little brother, his stomach churned and he nearly vomited.

“Jimmy, you all right?” Mr. Sordino asked.

“I’ll be fine,” he mumbled, his voice raspy and broken.

"The doctor, he say our boy needs to rest," Mrs. Sordino whispered. "He needs to get some strength back. He needs some time to let his little body fight back. You go for now."

"I don't want to leave him," he answered. "He wouldn't be here if I hadn't left him yesterday."

"Jimmy, you can't think that," Mr. Sordino said. "This place is bad. Full of bad people. Drunks on the streets. Blood on the sidewalks. Men killing men over a few miserable dollars. We've been lucky for many years."

"Jimmy," Mrs. Sordino interrupted. "You go for now. You go finda you friends," she said in a whisper. "Then, you boys finda the one who hurt my little Guisseppe and you make him pay for this horrible thing he do."

"Hazel!" Mr. Sordino shouted. "That's not the Lord's way. It's not our way. You can't put this on young Jimmy and his friends. I'll take care of this later."

"No. No. She's right, Mr. Sordino," he corrected. "It'll be okay if another boy goes after the one who did this. If a man goes after a boy and hurts him, then it's jail or worse. When I find him, it'll just be another fight. Only this time, I'll hurt him. I'll hurt him really bad."

CHAPTER TWENTY-ONE

Waiting together outside the hospital were Sarah, Eddie, and the rest of his gang. He joined them at the bottom of the stairs, still thinking about Mrs. Sordino asking for him to revenge Sordi's attack.

"We need to find who did this," he told them.

"I bet it was that thug Bruno and his gang," Eddie said.

"We need to be sure," he added. "Sordi said another name I'd never heard before."

"Who the hell else would beat a kid half-to-death and then dump the body at a loading dock?" Bobby ranted.

"Has anyone seen Bruno or his gang around here lately?" he asked.

They looked at one another shaking their heads. Then Bobby explained, "We came straight here as soon as we heard about Sordi."

"What'll you do when you find Bruno?" Sarah asked.

"Nobody does nothing until I say so," Skinner yelled. "Soon as you locate where he's holed up, you come get me. Don't do nothing on your own. And that includes you, Eddie."

"Yeah. Yeah. I hear you," Eddie answered. "I just want to talk to him." Then he smashed a fist into the palm of his other hand.

"Damn it, Slevin, I'm serious," he shouted. "I already got one friend in the hospital fighting for his life." *Sides, if anyone's gonna punish Bruno, it'll be me, he thought.*

"How's he doing?" Bobby asked.

"Not too good," he said. "Doctor says his jaw is broken and his ribs punctured his lung. Says it's hard for him to breathe, so he cut a hole in his neck and put a tube in it. Called it a 'traky-something'."

"I never heard of it; is it safe?" asked Jackie.

"My mom says this doctor is damn good, so I trust him for now," he answered.

"Is Jessie inside with your mother?" Sarah asked.

"Oh, no. I forgot all about her," he said. "She's working at the clinic today. I gotta get over there before she hears about Sordi from someone else."

"Mind if I go with you?" Sarah asked. "We need to talk about this business with Bruno."

"Sure, you can come," he replied. "But Bruno is my concern, not yours."

"Skinner, what do you want us to do?" Eddie asked.

"Eddie, you go find out where Bruno lives and see if he's still there," he directed. "He's the one we want. Not those punks in his gang."

"What about me and Jackie?" Bobby asked.

"Get over to the sheriff's office and find out what the hell they're doing about this," he ordered. "Don't tell them anything about Sordi being our friend. In fact, don't give them your real names."

"Why not?" Bobby asked.

"Because Bruno and his boys just might end up needing some medical attention of their own," he explained. "And we don't want any connection between them and us."

"Afternoon Mrs. Simonian," he said as he and Sarah entered the animal clinic.

"Hi, Skinner," she answered. "You looking for Jessie?"

"Yes ma'am, thank you. We need to see her as soon as possible."

"They're in the back working on a dog that had a run-in with a pack of coyotes," she explained. "You can go through here."

"Hello, Doctor Tom," he said. "We need to speak with Jessie for a few minutes, if that's okay?"

"What's happened?" his sister asked. "Is it Father? Mother? What is it?"

"Maybe it's best if we go outside for this," Sarah said and walked towards the back door.

"What is it Jimmy?" his sister begged. "Just tell me."

"Jessie, Sordi's been hurt," he said. "Someone beat him up real bad. Looks like maybe they used a club or something."

"Oh, my God, not my Guisseppe," she cried. "Where is he? Where is he?"

"St. Patrick's," Sarah answered. "He's still unconscious. Doctor Nelson says he may be that way for hours. Says he…."

His sister dropped the bandages she was holding for Doctor Tom and ran out the front door. He apologized for the intrusion and quickly explained what had happened. Then he and Sarah started back to the hospital.

"Jimmy, you need to let the sheriff handle this Bruno kid and his gang," Sarah started. "Sordi needs you to be there with him. Not off trying to find some punk to beat up."

"I have no intension of leaving him for any reason," he insisted.

"Then you'll let the law handle this?" she asked.

"You really shouldn't talk about something you don't understand," he cautioned.

"What's that supposed to mean?" Sarah asked.

"In Butte, if you're under 15 years old, the law looks at fighting as a sport," he began. "And, just like football or bareback riding, there's going to be a certain amount of accidents and injuries. And too bad if some kids end up dead."

"Are they crazy?" she shouted.

"Then, once a kid is 15 or older, it's against the law to fight," he explained.

"So that's a good thing," Sarah said. "The sheriff will arrest that kid. Won't he?"

"Well, answer me this," he said. "If Sordi throws the first punch, isn't Bruno acting in self-defense?"

She paused. "Well..."

"Well nothing," he exclaimed. "Since I wasn't there with Sordi, I can't prove Bruno threw the first punch. I can't prove Bruno had four guys hold Sordi while he beat him with a club. I can't prove Bruno planned this whole thing just to get to me!"

"Okay. Okay. I understand the chances the sheriff will do anything are slim," Sarah said. "But will you at least give them some time to investigate?"

"I told you, when we get back to St. Pat's, I'm not leaving Sordi for any reason."

"Jimmy?" she asked. "Do you know where it happened? Where they hurt Sordi?"

"He didn't say. I'd guess it was down by the creek."

"Maybe we can go there to see if anyone is hanging around. Maybe ask a few questions?" she offered.

"Thought you wanted the sheriff to take over," he said.

"I do," she replied slowly. "But he's my friend too, and if we can help the sheriff, then that's what I want to do."

As they approached the tailings mounds, Skinner motioned for Sarah to be quiet. "They still might be here," he whispered. "I'll climb up and take a quick look."

He scaled the 20-foot high mound and peered over the top. "No one here," he said. "Just some sandwich wrappers and a couple empty growlers. Looks like this might be the place. Seems only right, this is where Mrs. Sordino gets her wish."

CHAPTER TWENTY-TWO

As he approached the hospital entrance in a full run, he took the stairs three at a time. Out of breath, but not the least bit tired, he was excited about seeing his friend again. His momentum carried him past the nurses' station and half way up the hall towards the private room before someone yelled, "No visitors."

He stopped and turned to see a new young nurse he didn't know. "It's okay. I'm Kathryn O'Brien's son. She's helping Dr. Nelson."

"I'm sorry young man," she said. "No visitors until the doctor comes out and tells me it's okay."

"The doctor's in with my friend now?" he asked and then started to return to her desk."

"Yes, he is."

"Why?" he questioned.

"I don't ask why," she said. "Now, you're more than welcome to have a seat in the waiting area down by the cafeteria."

Before he could say another word, Sarah came running in. "How's he doing?"

"Can't go in until Doctor Nelson comes out," he said.

"Is he all right?" she asked.

"Yeah, I'm sure he is," Skinner asserted. Then he grabbed her hand and pulled her back towards the double-door entrance.

"What are you doing Jimmy?"

"My mother showed me a back way into the hospital this morning," he said.

They ran down the front steps and past the laundry building. Then they followed a small walkway around behind it to reach the alleyway. They continued back up to the wooden walkway his mother had used earlier and entered.

"I'll just take a quick look to see what's happening," he whispered. Then he turned the knob and pushed on the door.

"Kathryn, keep lifting his arms up and down. Roger, keep pushing on his chest," Dr. Nelson instructed. He moved his stethoscope in a small circle on Sordi's bare chest saying, "I still don't have a heartbeat."

"What did you say?" Skinner asked.

"Someone get him out of here," the doctor yelled.

"Mother? What's happening?" he demanded. She didn't answer, but continued to methodically raise and lower Sordi's bandaged arms over his head.

He glanced in the corner where the Sordinos were standing and crying.

"Jimmy," Sarah said and grabbed his arm. "Leave them alone. Let them do what they need to do." Then she pulled him back into the hall and closed the door.

He began to pace back and forth in front of Sordi's room. Sarah said nothing.

"His heart had stopped," his mother reported as she pushed open the door. "It's beating again." Then she motioned for the two of them to enter Sordi's room.

"Doctor Nelson, is he going to be all right?" Sarah asked.

"His breathing is getting worse," the doctor said softly.

"Well, what are you doing to help him?" he demanded.

"I'm doing everything I can, young man," Doctor Nelson snapped.

"Well, I can help." Skinner moved next to the bed and leaned down next to Sordi's bandaged covered left ear.

"Sordi. It's me, Skinner. I'm here. I'm with you, buddy," he shouted.

"Son, he can't hear you," the doctor chided.

"The hell he can't," he answered. Then he leaned closer and lowered his voice, "Sordi, you're the best friend I ever had. The brother I never had. We're friends forever. We have fish to catch. Grapes to grow."

"Skinner," Sarah said softly as she touched his arm.

He ignored her and continued, "Dammit, the gang needs you. Sarah needs you. Your parents need you. I need you." When he didn't respond, he gently laid his head on the bed next to Sordi' arm and sobbed openly.

After a few more minutes, he stood up and reached out for Sarah's hand. She joined him next to Sordi's bed. "Your son was very strong," the doctor said, looking at the Sordinos. "He fought all night long."

"Was? Was? Are you giving up?" Mr. Sordino questioned.

"I'm saying there's nothing more I can do for him. I was hoping he'd get stronger, but now it's time for you to let your son go," the doctor whispered.

"No. No. I'm a no letting my son go," Mrs. Sordino cried. She stood up and pounded her fist in her hand. "I'm a gonna fight for him. Just like he would fight for me. Like he would fight for you doctor! How come you no gonna fight for him anymore?"

"Hazel. That's enough," Mr. Sordino said. "Dr. Nelson has done everything he can for our Guisseppe."

"No. No. No. Not my little one. Not now. He's too young," she groaned.

Mr. Sordino reached out and held Dr. Nelson's right hand in his two hands. "You're a good man, doctor. We thank you for trying to save our son."

"Jeemy. Oh Jeemy," Mrs. Sordino cried. "Say good bye to your little brother."

Not knowing what else to do, Skinner decided to try one last thing. He reached down and gently grabbed his friend's left shoulder and shook it just a little. "Sordi. Sordi. It's me, Skinner. "I'm right by your side. I need you to wake up my little friend," he pleaded. "I have some good news. Bodie's alive."

Sordi moved his head slightly and opened the swollen, bright purple slit that used to be his left eye. It opened enough for him to see his best friend, his mother and father, and Sarah. Then Sordi smiled the smallest of smiles and mumbled something, his voice too raspy and strangled to understand.

"What did you say?" he asked. "I couldn't hear you." He leaned in closer.

Then, in a shallow, crackling voice, Sordi whispered, "You nodda gonna believe." And then he was gone.

CHAPTER TWENTY-THREE

With each long stride, the pain burned deeper in Skinner's gut and in his heart. He tried to fight back the anger, but soon lost all control of his emotions. By the time he slammed the hospital's back-door open, the tears flowed down his cheek as never before. Anger, guilt, and frustration churned together in his stomach as he kicked garbage cans and punched the building walls. When he finally stopped the destructive tirade, his bloodied fists fell to his side and he stared up at the grey metal sky. The volcano inside slowly erupted into a guttural, animal-like scream of total frustration.

"This has to be one of biggest funerals ever," Eddie said. "I'll bet there were more than 300 at the mass. Might even be more at the reception. We better keep moving."

"Sordi's dad is the best blacksmith within a hundred miles," Lynch added. "And his mom helps out down at the mission feeding the hungry. Hell, everyone likes the Sordinos."

"It's not right. This shouldn't have happened," he said. "I should have stayed with him to help him look for Bodie."

"There was no way you could have known those bastards had taken the dog," Bobby said.

"And who the hell kills a dog?" Jackie added. "Especially a dog that loves everyone."

"Everyone but you Jackie," Eddie quipped.

"Not today, Slevin," he replied. "No jokes today."

"Sorry Skinner, but Sordi wouldn't want us to be sad," Eddie answered back. "He was one happy kid, all the time. And by God, that's how I'm gonna remember him."

"Guess that's okay. We'll all handle this in our own way," he said. "I just can't think of anything except Sordi fighting that sum-bitch Bruno, and me at home eating supper."

"We've been to Bruno's shack four or five times since Monday and no one's ever there," Eddie said. "Me and Bobby even banged on his door last night around midnight. Still no answer."

"We'll find him," he added. "And when we do, he'll pay."

"So, Skinner. Where's Sarah?" Lynch asked. "I didn't see her at mass."

"She said she'd be better off helping get the reception ready," he replied. "I don't think she's too keen on churches."

As they approached the Italo-American Club, the line at the front door was already more than a block long. He walked his friends around back and came in through the kitchen. There were two long tables near the stage that were reserved for the Sordinos and the O'Briens.

"Hey, Skinner. There's your dad," Eddie yelled. The noise from all the people already inside was very loud.

"Hello, Mr. O'Brien," said Bobby. "Good to see you on a bad day."

"Hello boys," his father replied. "Before we get situated and involved in all this food and drink, I'd like you fellas to join me out back for a few minutes."

Slevin, Lynch and Murphy each looked at Skinner.

"Sure Dad. What's going on?" he asked.

His father didn't reply. He just stood and walked quickly across the huge hall and through the kitchen to the back door. When he was about 100 yards from the building he stopped, and waited until all four boys arrived and were standing close, facing him.

"Boys, I believe I know how much Sordi meant to you," his father began. "I believe I also know how much you're hurting. Even though I didn't know him for very long, I lost a very good friend in Stretch. It hurts. It hurts really bad."

"Sordi wasn't my friend," Skinner corrected. "He was my brother. You ever lose a brother?"

"No son, I haven't. But I've lost people I loved and loved dearly," his father replied. "This isn't about the pain we're all feeling. Or who's feeling worse than who. This is about doing the sensible thing. This is about making a mature decision to not go after the people who did this. The people who are clearly willing and able to kill each and every one of you."

"You want us to just forget about what happened to Sordi?" Eddie asked.

"No. Never forget. But this time, let the sheriff do his job. Let him and his deputies find these thugs and put them behind bars for the cowardly thing they did. Twenty-five years in prison will hurt a hell of a lot more than any beating you might give them."

"Do you really think the sheriff will do anything?" Bobby asked. "Hell, we been looking for three days and we can't find hide nor hair of them."

"Bobby!" Skinner yelled.

Bobby shrugged his shoulders and looked down at the ground.

"Son, I'm not stupid," his father said. "I know you. I know your first reaction is to strike back and hurt the ones who took your friend. But this time it isn't just a fist fight. If it was, I'd turn you loose with my blessing."

"Father, I don't know if I can wait for the sheriff to do his job. I don't know if I believe justice will be done."

"All I'm asking is for you guys to give it a chance. That's all," his father said. He reached out and put his hands on his shoulders. "Will you do that for me, son?"

Skinner hesitated just long enough to make it look as though he was thinking about his father's request. Then he said softly, "Yes, I think I can do that."

CHAPTER TWENTY-FOUR

Skinner couldn't help himself. He had to smile as he lay in bed reliving the last day he had spent with Sordi. He'd told a new joke about a man sitting behind a lady in church who gets punched in the eye for helping pull her dress from between her large cheeks as she stood up and sat down during an especially long mass. Then two weeks later, he was punched again when he helped her by pushing the dress back between her amble buttocks, assuming that's what she preferred. They both laughed until they cried. That was a week ago today.

"Jimmy?" his mother called. "Two boys are here to see you."

Already dressed, he rolled off his cot and walked to the front door. He was surprised to see two kids from Bruno's gang standing some twenty feet away from the house.

"What the hell do you want?" he asked.

"Name's Doc Emmert. He's Cecil Moore," the taller boy announced. "Weren't right what he did to your friend."

"You talkin about Bruno?"

"Naw. I'm talking about the big kid from Anaconda," the taller boy replied. "The one they call Stubbs."

"Stubbs? What kind of name is that?" he asked.

"He got his fingers cut off in an accident helping his father cut some timber for the smelter," the other kid answered. "Damnedest things you've ever seen. They're like black little hammers."

"So, Bruno wasn't behind all this?" he questioned.

"Yeah, it was Bruno's idea all right," Doc said. "He was so pissed when you whupped him on the 4th of July, he swore he'd find a way to get you back."

"Except he knew he couldn't beat you in fair fight," Cecil added.

"So, why are you here?" he asked.

"Bruno's pretty tough I guess, but he's really just a damn mean coward," Doc said. "He took off the next morning when he heard you took your friend to St. Pat's."

"Went to Colorado to live with his older cousin and work on building highways," Cecil explained.

"The three others in his gang went with him. Nobody wanted to go to no jail," Doc added.

"So why are you here?" he asked again.

"We're the ones who carried your friend and his dead dog to the loading dock," Doc began. He kept his eyes fixed on Skinner's every move. "We took good care of him all the way there. I even laid his dog there with him."

"Yeah, we left him a canteen of water and covered his legs with a blanket," Cecil said.

"We like a good fight," Doc said. "But this kid ain't no kid. Hell, he's bigger than either of us. And he's mean. Real mean."

"It wasn't a fair fight from the get-go," Cecil said. "Like a man fighting a kid."

"Yeah, but your friend sure hit him a lick," Doc added. "Damned if he didn't whack him off at the knees and drive him to the ground. Then he smacked him a couple times and cut his eye pretty good."

For just a moment, Skinner reveled in Sordi's attack. Then he returned to reality and asked, "So, Sordi hit him first?"

"Caught Stubbs by surprise, he did," Cecil said.

"So, I'll ask one last time—why are you here?"

"We've been lying low, but we heard the Sheriff ain't doin' nothing about what happened," Doc said. "We figure that bastard Stubbs ought to go to jail. Weren't no reason for him to go back and kick that kid in the ribs when he was already knocked out cold."

Skinner clenched his fists as the rage began to grow in his belly. "So, you want a medal for watching my best friend beat to death?"

"No. We just don't want to go to no jail," Cecil answered quickly. "We figure we help you find the bastard who did this—the right bastard, and you'll keep us out of it."

"Sides," Doc added. "This gives you a chance to go find that thug over in Anaconda and get some revenge."

"But you need to be careful with this one," Cecil warned. "This guy is big, mean and nasty. Really nasty. He killed your friend's dog just for fun."

"I think it's time for you boys to leave," he said. "I thank you for having the courage and the decency to come up here. I'll ask you to keep this information to yourself for now."

"You going to fight him?" Cecil asked.

He ignored the question and went back into the house. Within a few minutes, he was back out and headed to Eddie's house about a half mile away on the other side of Dublin Gulch.

He knocked on the door several times before Eddie finally answered. "What is it?" Eddie asked. "You don't usually come visiting on a Sunday."

"I need your help," he said sternly. "And I need it now."

"You find Bruno?"

"Bruno's gone," he snapped. "Ran like the miserable coward he is. Went to his cousin's place in Colorado. He won't be coming back this way any time soon. Sides, it wasn't Bruno that killed Sordi."

"Who the hell was it?" Eddie asked.

"Some big kid from Anaconda. They call him Stubbs."

"Jesus, Skinner," Eddie exclaimed. "That ain't no kid. I heard he's 16 or 17, and he's nothing but trouble. Hell, he killed some miner earlier this year."

"Why isn't he in jail?" he asked, already knowing Eddie's answer.

"Sheriff says the guy came looking for Stubbs because he had beaten up his brother the week before," Eddie said. "Sheriff says the kid threw the first punch. Makes it self-defense."

"I had two of Bruno's gang come up to my place this morning," he explained. "They're the ones who told me about Bruno leaving town and setting things up with this Stubbs kid. They also said Sordi knocked Stubbs on the ground first thing. Then he hit him a few more times and managed to cut his eye."

"Shit. Self-defense," Eddie said.

"This guy isn't going to no jail," Skinner said. "He ain't even going to court."

"What do we do?" Eddie asked.

"Would you go catch the noon supply train to Anaconda today and tell this thug I'm looking for him?" he asked. "Tell him I want to fight him tomorrow morning at 9 o'clock. He can catch the 8 o'clock train over from Anaconda."

"Are you sure?" Eddie asked.

"Would Sordi do it if it was me that got buried three days ago?"

"I'm on my way."

CHAPTER TWENTY-FIVE

Skinner had walked Sarah home many times and once, he had even met her parents and three brothers. Yet he'd never been inside their small rented home near the Diamond-Bell mine. He knew it wasn't far from Eddie's house, so he decided to make the twenty-minute walk and talk to Sarah. After standing on the small porch for several minutes gathering his courage, he finally knocked on the door.

"Good morning, young man," Mr. Grigsby said.

"Good morning, sir," he replied. "I'm sorry to bother you on a Sunday morning, but may I speak with Sarah? It's very important."

"Certainly. Come on inside," he said. "Mrs. Grigsby and the boys are at church. Me and Sarah aren't much for church going."

"Same goes for my father and me," he said.

"Morning, Jimmy. What are you doing here?" Sarah asked.

"Good morning, Sarah," he answered. "Could I talk with you for a few minutes?"

"Let's go out in back. There's a swing we can sit on."

They sat for several minutes, neither talking nor looking at the other. Finally, Sarah said, "Well, this can't be good."

"I know who killed Sordi."

"Was it that punk, Bruno?"

"No. It was some kid from Anaconda," he said.

"So, is the sheriff going after him?" Sarah asked.

"Nope. I am."

"Why you?"

"Sordi hit him first," he said. He stood and turned to look back at her. "That makes it self-defense. Technically, the kid didn't break the law."

"So, that makes it's all right for you to go and get yourself killed?"

"I'm not going to get killed," he replied. "I've fought lots of guys like Stubbs. Sure, they're big, strong, and mean. And they like to hurt smaller and weaker kids. I'm neither."

"Sordi wasn't weaker," she replied.

"Sordi was just too small," he said. "He couldn't hurt Stubbs enough by wrestling him to the ground. I know how to hurt him."

"Jimmy, we've only known each for a few weeks," Sarah began. "But I've already told you, I like you. A lot."

"I like you too."

"Let me finish," she said. "I like you, but that doesn't mean I want to marry you next month, or next year. I'm still just a kid growing up."

"Can I say something?" he asked.

"No. Not yet," she replied. "What I do know, is you're a good person. Some day you might even be a good husband. But that won't happen if some overgrown kid crushes your skull and kills you dead on the streets of this miserable town."

"Now, can I talk?" he asked.

"No," she said.

"I've already told you, I don't like Butte. Not the people, not the weather, not the smell, and most of all, not the mines," she announced. "But what I do like is you. You and your family."

"My turn?" he asked impatiently.

"Yes."

"Look, I'm not asking you to marry me either," he began.

"That's good," she said quickly.

"Hell, my parents didn't marry until they were 20 years old."

"Mine married at 17," she interrupted.

"Let 'me' finish," he snapped. "There are so many places I want to see. So many things I want to do before I find a good wife, have a mess of kids, maybe a dog, and then finally settle down. But that doesn't mean you're not the one I'll marry, someday."

"So, let this kid be," she said. "Let him find someone else to fight and hurt. Let him live his life and let us get on with ours, whatever that means."

"That's just it," he answered as he leaned closer. "If I let him go unchallenged and unpunished, he's going to do this again. And again. I can't let it go. Not for my father or my mother, or even for you. And especially not for Sordi. I have to try to put an end to this kid's fighting."

Sarah sat for a moment without saying anything. Then she asked, "When are you going to do this?"

"Sarah, it's no place for you to be," he said.

"No. Hell no," she shouted. "Don't you dare think I'm going to let you do this without me. I'm going to be there. You just won't see me until it's over. Now, when is this going to happen?"

He sat for a few moments without saying anything. Then he said, "I guess you're right. It's tomorrow morning around 9 o'clock."

"Where?" she asked.

"Same place we thought he fought Sordi," he said. "Eddie's headed over to Anaconda to set it up. He'll have Bobby and Jackie with him tomorrow, just in case things get out of control."

"Jimmy? If for some reason, any reason, you change your mind tonight, you must know we'll all feel better," she said. "But if you wake up tomorrow morning and know this is something you must do, then do it with every ounce of your skill and strength, and beat this miserable animal senseless."

CHAPTER TWENTY-SIX

During the night, he had tried to convince himself this was just another fight. Sure, this kid was bigger and maybe tougher than most. But he'd fought more than 100 times over the past two years and never lost. He'd never suffered more than a black eye, bloody nose, or a few minor cuts. And he'd sure as hell, never, ever, been on the verge of giving up. He could do this. If only he could talk to his father first.

"Jimmy, breakfast is ready," his mother called.

"Mornin' Mother," he said. Then he took his usual seat at the table and began to eat his oatmeal, toast, and milk.

"Where's Father working this week?" he asked.

"He'll be at the Parrot mine for at least a month," his mother answered. "It's the one on the southern edge of town, not far from *The Daily Post*."

He finished eating and carried his dishes to the sink for his mother to wash. Same as he always did. Nothing out of the ordinary this morning. Yet when it was time for him to head down to the newspaper, he couldn't stop himself from exchanging the normal "see you tonight, mother" for a quick kiss on the cheek and a soft "I love you, Mother."

"Well, that was a nice surprise," his mother said. "For that you get a peach cobbler tonight."

Eddie, Bobby, and Jackie were all waiting for him at the loading dock. No one was smiling.

"Hey, Gus," Skinner yelled as he approached. "The boys and I got a fight this morning. Give our papers to guys from Meaderville."

"Will do," Gus yelled back. "Hey O'Brien. Kick his ass and get back here tomorrow morning."

"Will do."

They had a couple of hours before the fight so they wandered down towards the creek to rest in the shade and talk about what was going to happen.

"Boys, I'm gonna say something and I don't want any argument," he began. "No matter what happens this morning, it ends here. No matter what."

"You'll be kicking his arse," Bobby said. "That's what's gonna happen."

"This fight isn't about me winning or losing," he said. "I'm here to punish this kid for what he did to Sordi. Be it a little or a lot, it's all we're gonna do from now on. After today, it's over."

"I ain't worried," Eddie added. "Yeah, he's big. But you fought bigger guys than him. We're just gonna make sure this one's a fair fight. When he starts to get his ass whipped, he might be looking for a little help."

"Is he bringing some guys with him?" Jackie asked.

"Yeah. The guys from Bruno's gang said he always has four or five that run with him."

For more than an hour the boys just sat there not saying much of anything. Finally, Skinner announced, "Let's get this over. We don't want the word to spread and end up with a bunch of townies."

The fight area was about a quarter mile from the creek. It had been used for local fights ever since the Silver Dollar Mine had closed some five years earlier. Surrounded by tailings mounds, the large, flat circular area in the middle made for a natural arena. He had never fought here, but he had seen several fights over the past few years.

As they approached the area, he heard it before he saw it: the sound of hundreds of people.

"What the hell is this?" he asked. "We only told Jimmy a couple hours ago."

"Um. I might have mentioned it to a few kids down at the Emporium last night after Eddie got back from Anaconda," Bobby admitted.

"Me too," Jackie added. "Didn't think you'd mind having a crowd for a big win."

"Jesus, Mary and Joseph," he mumbled.

"There he is," Eddie announced from atop one of the mounds. "He's the one with the growler of beer on the far edge of the circle."

They stood in silence watching for a few more seconds. Then they pushed their way down the face of the mound and through the crowd.

"Skinner. Skinner. Skinner." The chants from a clearly biased crowd were so loud it was hard for him to focus on his large, filthy-looking opponent dressed in all black, including a neck-to-ground black duster.

He slowly searched the crowd for Sarah. When he couldn't find her, he moved into the center of the circle and signaled he was ready to begin. The cheers rang out even louder than before. *A damn circus is all this was. And, he was the dancing bear.*

Stubbs didn't move. Instead, he just nodded to him and then downed the remainder of his beer.

"You come here to fight or drink?" Skinner yelled as he moved close enough for Stubbs to hear.

"Both," a red-haired kid standing next to Stubbs yelled back. Then Stubbs handed off the empty metal bucket, removed the duster and moved towards Skinner.

As Stubbs raised his hands into fighting position, Skinner saw for the first time the reason for his opponent's nick name. A shudder that started in his throat ran all the way down to his stomach. The blacked, calloused stumps were terrifying. Stubbs watched his opponent take a step back.

"You afraid of my little friends?" Stubbs asked. Then he lowered his hands to waist high and pounded the stumps into each other five or six times. And then he grinned.

Always the aggressor, Skinner began circling to his right. Generally awkward for most right-handed fighters, Skinner made it work by often leading with a straight right punch, instead of the more common left jab. It also moved him away from Stubbs' powerful right hand. And it made him reach further.

"You gonna dance or fight?" Stubbs asked.

"Both." Then he quickly snapped a crisp left jab and a stinging straight right into Stubbs' nose, drawing first blood.

The roar from the crowd was almost deafening.

Stubbs stopped circling as he let some of the blood trickle into his mouth. He smiled and then wiped the rest away on the long sleeve of his black shirt.

"That all you got punk?" Stubbs yelled.

"It's a start," he answered. Then he started circling to his left, hoping to keep Stubbs off balance.

Next came a series of left jabs that continued to batter Stubbs' bleeding nose. He knew this was only a distraction to this big kid and to win, he'd eventually have to move in closer.

Yet it was Stubbs who took the initiative and lunged forward, swinging wildly with his right. He easily ducked underneath and seized the opening with a quick step in closer. Two powerful hooks, one left and one right, pummeled Stubbs' ribs, producing a groan heard by many. Again, the partisan crowd cheered wildly for their local hero.

Feeling good with his early success and control of the fight, Skinner began to feel he could win this fight. All he needed to do was stay away from Stubbs' massive right hand and he could wear him down. Carrying around some 200 pounds in the ever-increasing heat would soon add to Stubbs' problems.

"Damn. You're pretty good," Stubbs said. "Sure a lot better than your little wop friend I killed last week."

"You shut your filthy mouth about him. He was twice the man you'll ever be!"

"Hell, I fought tougher kids when I was eight years old. And they was bigger, too," Stubbs said with a laugh.

"You miserable sum bitch," he yelled. "You're gonna pay for that. You're going pay real good."

He knew Stubbs was taunting him so he'd make a mistake, but he didn't care. The blinding rage he had struggled to put out of his mind came flooding back. Just like the night of the 4th of July. And he was beginning to lose control.

"And what about that miserable excuse for a dog," Stubbs continued. "Too stupid to keep away from strangers. Glad I killed him too."

That was it. He couldn't hold back any more. He stepped in close and caught Stubbs as he tried to finish his threat. A straight right connected on the already broken nose. Blood flew in all directions. Then a sharp left hook, followed by a powerful right hook slammed into either side of Stubbs' already bloodied face. He hit him, and hit him, and hit him again.

Yet, instead of backing up or using his arms to cover his face, Stubbs just ignored his blows and unleashed a short, stinging left jab with the blackened, calloused nubs, catching Skinner on his right eye, splitting open the bushy brown eyebrow. The blood flowed down and instantly clouded his vision. Without a pause, Stubbs connected with a crushing roundhouse right hook that caught him just under his left arm. He felt the paralyzing pain a split second before he heard his ribs crack. His legs weakened and sent him crashing to his knees.

Unable to catch his breath or fight off the pain, he was relieved to see Stubbs back off and walk over to the edge of the ring. He watched as the arrogant bastard laughed with the crowd and then reached for another growler of beer.

He needed to focus. He needed to breathe. He needed to survive.

"Just what I thought," Stubbs yelled. "You can't hold your mud." The crowd near him cheered and began chanting, "Stubbs. Stubbs. Stubbs."

Skinner knew he was in trouble. He also believed he could still win this fight with a little luck and a plan. They each knew he had some broken ribs on his left side. When they faced off again, Stubbs would expect a punch from his right – still his strongest weapon. If he could mask the pain he knew would come, a well-placed left hook just might shatter Stubbs' already battered nose and maybe end the fight. It was his only chance.

As he finally got back up to his feet, Stubbs yelled, "You ready punk?" He still had the beer in his left hand. "Be with you directly." Then he drained the growler and threw it on the ground.

He'd only get one chance to pull this off. He leaned forward and to his left, as if he was protecting his left side. Stubbs grinned and marched straight for him, raising his hands into fighting position. He waited until Stubbs was right on top of him and then he drew back his right fist. Stubbs dropped his right hand slightly as he raised his left to block the oncoming blow. His face was an open target on the right. He released a fierce left hook with all his might. Just inches short of its target, the left arm stopped instantly and then recoiled back away from Stubbs face.

"Noooooo," he screamed and reached across his body with his right hand. There, he found the jagged end of a broken rib bone sticking through the skin and his blood-drenched shirt. Again, his legs failed him and he fell back to a kneeling position.

"Say good night you little bastard," Stubbs said as he moved in and delivered a powerful roundhouse right to Skinner's left cheek.

The next thing he heard was the muffled sound of the crowd cheering for Stubbs. He was lying face down on the ground, his head in a pool of warm blood. He started to move but the pain from his broken rib was too much. Then, as he struggled more and more to breathe, he had no choice but to push through the pain and roll over on his back. He could not hold back the scream. The crowd stopped their chanting.

"Well, well, well," Stubbs said. He walked over and stared down. "Does it hurt my little friend?"

Paralyzed in pain, Skinner could only stare up at the animal who was about to end his life.

Stubbs bent down closer, so only Skinner would hear. "Do you think the little wop felt pain like this before I killed him?"

"You go straight to hell," Skinner gasped.

"No, I think I'll send you there first." Then Stubbs sat down and straddled Skinner's legs. He pushed and played with the protruding rib bone, smiling as Skinner screamed over and over. Then he slapped Skinner's blood covered face with his right hand and then the same with his left.

His cheek lying over against the ground, Skinner could see the crowd beginning to leave. He wished he could see Sarah. "Before you go, just remember who threw the first punch today," Stubbs said. He leaned down, straightened his face, and stared him in the eyes. "This is all legal. Ain't no law ever gonna touch me. Not now. Not ever."

Stubbs grinned a sickly grin as he coiled his massive right hand for a final punch. Then he stopped. The smile disappeared. His right hand fell limply back to his side. He stared straight down at him, but neither said nor did anything. Blood began to seep out between his lips and down his chin. And then, as Skinner watched Stubbs fall over onto the ground, everything went black.

CHAPTER TWENTY-SEVEN

He ran to his son as fast as he could. His boy's blue denim shirt was covered in blood from his chest to his waist. He could see the tip of a jagged bone sticking through it just above the waist.

"James. James," he wailed. "Oh God, please be alive."

"Is he…?" Sarah asked as she reached the two men. "Is he, alive?"

"Send someone to get a doctor," he directed.

"Jackie Lynch!" she yelled. "You run as fast as you can to get a doctor."

Then someone in the crowd behind her yelled, "To hell with a doctor, someone get the sheriff."

Another voice said, "He did it. He did it. I saw him do it."

"Grab him. He killed that kid in cold blood," another spectator bellowed.

He heard the yells but ignored them. He wasn't leaving his son until the doctor arrived.

"James," he said softly. "It's your father. I'm right here with you. I won't leave your side."

He cradled his son's body in his arms and rocked gently back and forth. He continued to whisper assurances that he was there and wouldn't let anything harm him. Sarah sat on the ground across from him and appeared to be praying. Eddie and Bobby joined them and sat on either side of his son.

"Thank you, Sarah, for coming to the mine," he said looking at her with tears in eyes. "If you hadn't…"

"I was wondering why you weren't here this morning, Sarah," Eddie interrupted. "Skinner was asking about you."

Sarah ignored Eddie's comment and asked, "Mr. O'Brien, what's going to happen to you?"

"Don't worry about me, child," he answered. "You make sure James gets to the hospital as fast as he can. Stay with him until Dr. Nelson arrives."

"What about Mrs. O'Brien?" she continued.

"Don't leave James' side until Dr. Nelson sees him," he said. "Kathryn will get the news soon enough in the laundry."

"What should I tell her about you?"

"Tell her to stay with James. I'll be fine."

"Fine? Fine? What's that supposed to mean?" she snapped. "Do you have a lawyer? Do you even know a lawyer? They're gonna hang you."

"Child," he said shaking his head. "They'll probably take me to jail for a few hours and then release me. Hell, the bastard was trying to kill my son."

"I don't think they're going to see it that way," Eddie said. "A grown man threw a pickaxe into the back of a 16-year-old boy's head and killed him instantly. Sounds more like cold blooded murder."

Just then, two large young black men dressed in all white uniforms came running up to them. They glanced at the boy lying on the ground a few feet away with the pickaxe stuck in the back of his skull and one of them said, “He’s dead. What about the other one?”

“He’s alive,” Sarah yelled.

They moved quickly and efficiently and had James on the stretcher in less than a minute. Then they lifted it off the ground and sprinted back towards town.

“They aren’t going to run all the way back to the hospital, are they?” asked Sarah.

“Naw. They got a 1916 Model T ambulance parked about a hundred yards away,” Bobby said. “Damn thing will go almost 50 miles an hour. They’ll have Skinner at the hospital in less than five minutes.”

“Thanks, everyone,” he said. “Now you all get to the hospital and please, please stay with my son.”

A group of about 20 men were standing in a circle around him and the kids. He assumed they were making sure he didn’t leave before someone from the sheriff’s department arrived. He made no attempt to follow the orderlies and his son.

“Are you Sam O’Brien?” came a deep voice from behind him.

He turned and saw two deputies approaching, their guns drawn and hanging at their sides.

“Yes. I’m Sam O’Brien.”

“Put your hands behind you,” the larger of the two deputies directed. “You’re under arrest.”

“What’s the charge?” he asked, as he turned to face the two men.

“We don’t need a charge to take you in,” said the larger of the two.

“I’m guessing it’ll be murder. First degree murder,” snarled the smaller man, as his smile revealed a silver front tooth.

Sam did as he was told without any resistance or argument. He had no intention of fighting or trying to escape. There’d been enough fighting for today.

CHAPTER TWENTY-EIGHT

Jackie had remained at the hospital after summoning the ambulance. He was standing outside at the foot of the steps when Sarah and the boys approached the hospital.

"He's already in the emergency room," Jackie reported. "Doc Nelson's taking care of him right now."

"You guys stay here," she instructed. "I need to go find Skinner's mother."

"No, you don't," Jackie said. "She went running by me in the hallway just after they brought Skinner in. I think she's in the emergency room with the doc and Skinner."

Sarah continued to take charge and quickly organized the gang's activities. No one seemed to object.

"Eddie, would you run down to Doctor Tom's and let Jessie know what's happening?" she asked.

"Sure thing," he said. "Shall I bring her back here?"

"Please, as soon as you can."

"What can I do to help, Sarah?" Bobby asked. "Should I go tell Mr. Sordino?"

"No," she said. "Not until we find out how Jimmy's doing."

"What else can I do?" he asked again.

"Would you and Jackie go down to the jail?" she asked.

"Sure, but why."

"Find out as much as you can about what's happening with Mr. O'Brien," she said. "Ask if they're going to keep him. If they are, ask where they're gonna keep him. What's the charge? When will he go before the judge? Talk to as many people down there as you can."

"They're going to hang him," Jackie stated flatly.

"What the hell did you say?" Eddie asked.

"Kill a kid and you going to die," Jackie replied. "Lived here long enough to know it's always been that way."

"Shut your mouth!" shouted Eddie. "You don't know what the hell you're talking about." He took a couple of steps closer to Jackie, who didn't move.

"Easy boys," she said. "We can't let our emotions get the best of us. We need to help our friends, not fight amongst ourselves."

The two boys stood toe-to-toe and stared at each other for a few moments longer. Then Jackie said, "Sorry, Eddie. I should just keep my big mouth shut."

"Ah, it's all right," Eddie replied. "She's right. We need to stick together."

Jackie turned, grabbed Bobby's arm and said, "Let's go, Bobby," and they headed off down the street.

"Hey, Jackie," she yelled. "See if you can find a reporter still hanging around down there. He'll be asking all the right questions. Stick close to him."

"I can do that," he yelled back as he and Bobby walked quickly down the street.

She approached the nurses' station and asked the first one she came to, "Is there any news on Jimmy O'Brien?"

"Nothing yet, miss," said a young, thin woman with bright red hair and a face full of freckles. "Please, have a seat and I'll go take a quick look."

"You'll do no such thing," boomed a deep voice from behind her. "You'll get upstairs and check on the patients that need you. Not some street thug who's always fighting."

Sarah recognized the older heavy-set nurse from last week. She chose not to confront her and retreated to the waiting area.

Before she found a seat, she heard, "Sarah?" She turned to see Kathryn walking quickly towards her.

"How's Jimmy Doing?" she asked.

"Not very good," Kathryn blurted out. "It's worse than what happened to Sordi. There was a terrible blow to his left cheek that has caused his brain to swell."

"Oh my God," she gasped. Then she took a deep breath and asked, "That sounds bad. But what does it mean?"

"It means I need to go see Sam right away," Kathryn said. "Doctor Nelson says Jimmy won't make it through the night if he doesn't operate right away."

"Has Doctor Nelson ever done this kind of operation?" she asked.

"I don't think so," Kathryn replied. Then she held up a piece of paper and said, "That's why I need to see Sam. We both must sign this waiver that says we won't hold Doctor Nelson responsible if anything goes wrong."

"You mean if he kills Jimmy," she corrected.

"If we don't let him try, we might as well put a gun to Jimmy's head," Kathryn snapped back. "I've seen this kind of injury before and there's no other option. Do nothing and he will die."

"Of course, you're right, Kathryn. I'm sorry I said that."

Kathryn grabbed Sarah's shoulders and looked her straight in the eyes. "God help me child, but I'm going to leave my son right now because I must. I want you to go and be with him. Do not, for any reason, leave his side until I return. Do you understand me?"

In a calm and reassuring voice, she said, "No matter what, I will not leave his side. I promise."

Kathryn was hurrying towards the front door when she stopped, turned, and quickly walked back to the nurses' station. Staring at young woman with the red hair, she announced, "This young lady is part of my family. She's going stay with my son until I return." She didn't wait for any reply.

CHAPTER TWENTY-NINE

When Sarah had come running to the mine, frantically begging him to come stop a fight, he knew his son had ignored his warnings and was trying to get revenge for his best friend's murder. What he didn't know was he would have to take a life to save his son's life. If he had, he would have done the same thing that put him here.

"Get your stupid arse up there, you pathetic child killer," sneered one of the deputies. Then, before he could react, the deputy shoved him up the two steps and into the wagon. With his hands in cuffs behind him, Sam couldn't balance himself and promptly fell face first onto a floor that smelled of stale beer, vomit, and excrement.

"Would you be wantin' to stop off on the way to jail and kill a few dogs and cats, you arsehole," the other deputy added.

He quickly retreated inside his mind, thinking only of his son and how he wanted to be with him at the hospital. How he would hold him and tell him how much he loved him. And when he was at young Sordi's funeral, how his father John had lamented how painful it was that he hadn't had a chance to tell his son how much he loved him before he passed away. That same pain was tearing him apart right now.

"Time to visit your new home," said a guard. They had reached the sheriff's office and jail and were taking him inside. As soon as he climbed down the stairs of the wagon and onto the street, one of the deputies kicked him hard in the butt. Again, he fell face-first onto the cement sidewalk and scrapped the right side of his face. He felt the blood starting to ooze down his face.

"Please watch your step, kind sir," the guard warned and then laughed. Then, without waiting for him to get back to his feet, they grabbed his shoulders and dragged him into the sheriff's office.

Robert Johansen had been Butte's only sheriff for the past 20 years. The city's most seasoned deputy at the time, he was the recipient of a field promotion at 12:01 AM on January 1st, 1900, when someone's celebratory bullet fell back to earth and killed then-sheriff James Favini. The two of them had been standing in the middle of Main Street exchanging New Year's best wishes.

Sam had heard plenty of rumors that Johansen was honest, but brutal. He showed little or no mercy for anyone unlucky enough to end up in his jail. He had said on many public occasions, "If you're arrested, you're guilty." He tried to prepare for the worst.

"Get this filthy coward out of my sight," Johansen yelled. He pointed towards the floor and added, "Take him to cell 1A. Let's see how he likes it down there after a few weeks."

The deputies pulled him towards a large, grey metal door at the back of the office and one of his escorts swung it open. The other pushed him down the dark, narrow stairway and he immediately lost his footing. He tumbled downward for several seconds, landing on his back, his feet still stuck in the stairwell.

"I warned you, sir," laughed one of the deputies as walked down the stairs. "You'll need to be a little more careful in the future."

As they yanked him to his feet, he quickly scanned the dimly lit area for some point of reference. It appeared to be a small dungeon with the same wretched smell from the paddy wagon. Only this time the temperature was sweltering and the air was smothering.

"We reserve this suite for only our best guests," a deputy said. "In case you're wondering, the last guy who stayed here was hung for killing his wife and her mother."

"If my wife's mother lived in Butte, I'd probably end up down here too," the other deputy said. They both laughed as one of them opened the door to a small cell.

"Hold still if you want your cuffs unlocked," a deputy snapped. "I got to get outta here before I puke." He slammed the cell door, locked it, and ran for the stairway.

"What happens next?" he yelled.

"You'll go in front of a judge tomorrow morning," one of them replied as they hurried up the stairs.

"I need to speak with an attorney," he shouted.

"The ol' bastard will be here in a couple hours," came the faint reply from upstairs.

Then the door at the top of the stairs slammed shut and silence replaced all the commotion. He couldn't hear anything from the office above. What sounds he could hear were what he assumed were rats scurrying around the edges of his new home.

He continued to survey his surroundings as he tore a piece of his blue denim work-shirt to cover his nose. The combination of the smell, stagnant air and unbearable heat made him nauseous and dizzy. He scanned the floor for a place to sit. There was no cot or chair, only a thin, dark grey mattress lying on the cement floor. He slumped down and tried to stretch his legs. The toes of his boots reached the far wall before they could straighten.

The door at the top of the stairs opened back up after just a few minutes. Maybe he was right and they realized it was only a father trying to save his son's life. Maybe this horrible nightmare was already over.

"Sam? Sam?" came the voice from the office above. "Sam, it's me, Kathryn."

"No. Don't come down," he yelled back.

"Sam, it's about Jimmy?!" she replied as she started down the worn, narrow stairway.

"Is he okay?"

She didn't answer, but continued to walk towards him. "Katy, is James alive?" Sam asked.

She approached the cell as he stood to face her. "Yes, he is. But he needs an operation," she explained.

"So, tell them to do it. Pay them whatever it takes," Sam said.

"It's not about the money," she said. "It's about time."

"What are you saying?"

"Jimmy's brain is swelling and Doctor Nelson says he needs an operation today. He's never done this kind, but he knows he can't wait for the doctor from Billings. He has to operate right now."

"You know him better than I do," Sam began. "What do you think we should do?"

"We need to sign this paper that gives him our permission. Right now."

Without another word, he took the paper and pencil from her and scribbled his signature at the bottom. Then he pushed it back through the bars.

"He'll been fine," Sam said. "Remember, your mother said he has the heart of wolf."

"I hope she was right," she said. "This'll be the toughest fight of his life."

"Kathryn. I'm sorry you had to come down here," he said and looked deep into her eyes. "Not the nicest place to bring a lady, what with the smell and all."

"Sam, my love," she replied with a smile. "Are you forgetting where I work? You want bad smells? Come to work with me some day."

"If I get the chance, I most certainly will."

CHAPTER THIRTY

The jail was six long blocks from the hospital. As Katy hurried along the sidewalk she tried to stay calm and focused on the task at hand. And yet, all she could think of was the scene with Sordi just one week ago. She struggled to push the memory from her consciousness and increased her walk to a run.

"Doctor Nelson, I have the release," she said as she entered the emergency room.

The doctor took the release and without looking to see if it was signed, handed it to the nurse on his left. "I assumed Mr. O'Brien would agree," Doctor Nelson said. "We're ready to operate."

"Aren't you going to move him into the operating room?" she asked.

"No, everything we need is right here," he answered. "The procedure is relatively simple, but extremely dangerous."

"Cutting open my son's skull and brain is a simple procedure?"

"I'm not going to do any such thing," he said. "I've spoken with Doctor Radnitz in Billings and he advised me to make slight incision and insert a small tube through the skull to drain the excess fluid. It's called an extraventricular shunt."

"Will Doctor Radnitz be coming to Butte tomorrow?" she asked. "In case there are complications?"

"No."

She waited for him to explain further. He didn't. "What do you mean, no?"

"Kathryn, every minute we talk, the more fluid James' body produces and pumps into his skull," Doctor Nelson said. "If I don't insert this tube now, he'll die. If I do it correctly, the danger is over. If I don't, then the danger is over. No need for Dr. Radnitz."

"I'm sorry, doctor," she whispered. "I believe you can do this procedure. I believe you will save my boy's life."

"Thank you, Kathryn," Doctor Nelson said. "I should be out to see you in about an hour."

When she turned to walk out, she noticed Sarah standing in the corner. "I forgot all about you child," she said. "Are you all right?"

"He's strong, Mrs. O'Brien," Sarah said. "He'll fight for all he's worth."

"I know he will," she replied and walked over and embraced her. "Now let's go outside and let the doctor do what he needs to do."

They were about to sit down on a bench in the hallway just down from the emergency room entrance, when Jessie ran in and hugged her.

"Mother. Mother, is he alive?" Jessie cried.

"Yes child, he's in the emergency room with Doctor Nelson," she said. "The doctor's going to do a small operation that will help Jimmy get better."

Her arm still around Jessie's shoulders, she guided them to the bench and they sat. Sarah also put her arm around Jessie's waste and the three of them sat together in silence.

Finally, she was about to speak when she heard someone say, "Mrs. O'Brien?"

She turned and soon recognized it was James' teacher. "Hello, Mrs. Camp."

"Hello," she replied. "I don't mean to bother you at a time like this, but James is such a special boy. I just had to see how he was doing."

"It's a serious head injury, Mrs. Camp," she said. "Doctor Nelson is performing an emergency operation right now."

"Please, call me Dorothy. Is there anything I can do?"

"Pray. Pray for both my son and my husband," she said.

"I came as soon as I heard," Dorothy replied.

"Thank you so much," she said. "James loved being in your class. He couldn't wait to get to school. Don't think I've ever seen a child so unhappy about summer vacation."

"In all my years of teaching, James is truly unique," Dorothy said. "And I told him so."

"What do you mean, unique?"

"James has a gift that combines intelligence with compassion and curiosity," Dorothy said. "And yet, he's capable of such violence and destruction, it makes me wonder if he's really two people sharing the same body."

"He wasn't like this when we lived on the farm," she said. "He was the sweetest child ever, who loved to read and go exploring."

"Butte has ruined many a young boy," Dorothy lamented. "I would hate to see James become just another statistic. I already know one of those."

"It hasn't done much for my Sam, either."

"Speaking of Sam, do you have an attorney?" Dorothy asked.

"Sheriff Johansen said there's a local attorney that helps folks like us with little or no money," she replied. "Says his name is Robert Barr and he's very experienced."

"Oh, my lord, you can't use him," Dorothy quickly protested. "Bones is almost seventy years old and hasn't won a case in 20 years."

"Bones?" she asked.

"Besides being old, that six-foot man can't weigh more than 150 pounds soaking wet," Dorothy answered. "Folks been callin' him Bones for 30 years or more."

"Well, skinny or not, he can surely win this one. Sam was just trying to save our son's life."

"Don't be so naïve, Kathryn," Dorothy scolded. "Your cowardly husband killed a defenseless young boy by throwing a pickaxe into the back of his head. A boy who was—as I heard it—just fighting in self-defense."

"The hell you say," she shouted and stepped closer to the woman. "My Sam would never…"

"That's not me saying that," Dorothy interrupted. "That's what the district attorney will be telling a jury filled with mothers and fathers."

She slumped back down onto the bench and sighed, "Oh no, I never thought about it that way. What am I going to do?"

"I know you've probably heard stories about my brother, Clayton," Dorothy began. "Stories that say he's a drunk and lives off my income, in my home."

"Yes, I've heard that on several occasions," she replied.

"But have you heard he was once one of the finest defense attorneys in San Francisco?"

"No. I have not."

"Well, he was," Dorothy said with obvious pride. "And, he was wealthy. Very wealthy."

"What happened?" she asked.

"A woman. She tore out his heart and broke his spirit."

"And that's the man I want fighting for my husband's life?"

"I've seen him in the courtroom here in Butte," Dorothy said. "He's the best around when he believes in the defendant."

"Do you really think he can save Sam?"

"I believe Clayton is your only hope," Dorothy said. "If we can just keep him sober until after the trial."

"And if we can't?"

"Even drunk, he's still a better attorney than Bones."

CHAPTER THIRTY-ONE

As the one-hour Doctor Nelson had promised turned into two, Kathryn began to question her quick decision to allow him to operate on her son. Had she taken the coward's way out by signing a one-page note that said, "Do what you will to my son"?

Her eyes were trained on the emergency room doors, waiting impatiently for any sign of movement. Finally, after two hours and seventeen minutes, an orderly swung the double doors open. She jumped to her feet and hurried to see what was happening. Doctor Nelson met her at the doorway.

"He's doing much better. The operation went as planned."

"Can I see him?" she asked.

"We're moving him to the room across from my office," he said. "He's still unconscious, but his vital signs are improving."

"Please doctor, just let me see his face," she begged.

"Certainly." He turned and motioned to the orderly to stop the gurney by the doorway.

"Oh, my God, no!" she gasped in horror as she looked down at her son. His head and face were bandaged exactly like Sordi's.

"He's not young Sordino," Doctor Nelson said as he reached out and steadied her. "He's doing much better. The swelling has already gone down some and he's breathing just fine."

"Oh, Jimmy," she said. She gently stroked his bandaged cheek and wept openly.

Sarah stood next to her and said nothing. Then she put her arm around Kathryn and said, "He needs to rest. He's going to be fine."

The doctor gave the signal for the orderly to move the gurney. She and Sarah returned to the bench and sat down. Doctor Nelson followed.

"Kathryn, Sarah, I don't want you to be misled," he said. "The operation was successful in that the shunt was inserted properly and is draining the excess fluid. However, he's not completely out of danger."

"How soon will you know?" Sarah asked.

"It may take 24 to 36 hours before he wakes up," Doctor Nelson said. Then he just stared at Kathryn.

"You mean he's going to live, but you don't know if Jimmy will be in there when his body wakes up," she said.

"Yes. That's exactly what I mean. We'll just have to wait and see."

"Well, no need for us to stay here," Sarah announced. "Let's go see if we can find your new attorney."

"What? What are you saying?" she asked.

"Doctor, you said Jimmy's going to live, didn't you?" Sarah asked.

"Yes, I believe he's in no real, life-threatening danger any longer," Doctor Nelson replied. "All he needs right now is lots of oxygen and an IV for nourishment. He should remain unconscious for the next 24 hours or so."

"Well, then," Sarah continued. "It's time to save Mr. O'Brien."

"Well, I, a, um, guess you're right," she stuttered in agreement. "How shall we find him?"

"The telephone directory," Sarah stated.

Within 15 minutes they were headed three blocks away to the northern edge of Butte, in a rundown section with a dozen small office buildings. On one of the worst was mounted a swinging wooden sign that read, "Clayton Camp, Attorney at Law."

Sarah knocked on the front door. There was no answer.

"It's Saturday. He's probably not in," she said. "I'll come back Monday."

"I heard what Mrs. Camp said about her brother being a drunk," Sarah said. "I'll bet you two bits he's in there passed out."

"I beg your pardon, young lady. I am not drunk. Not yet." The door had opened about halfway and a tall, slender man with silver hair and a matching moustache stood staring back at them. He was dressed in a grey suit with a white shirt and black tie that had seen their better days. And he was barefoot.

"We need to speak with you about representing her husband," Sarah said and pointed to Kathryn.

"Your name, madam?"

"Kathryn O'Brien."

"And is your husband, Samuel O'Brien?"

"Yes, he is," she answered. "How did you know?"

"Please, come in, come in," he replied and disappeared into the dimly lit office. "I make it a practice to have lunch every Saturday at a small café next to the sheriff's office. Lots of legal activity as a result of Friday night celebrations."

"How much do you charge?" Sarah asked. She remained outside and grabbed Kathryn's arm to hold her in place.

"So much for the pleasantries," he said and reappeared in the doorway. "I charge $500 to take the case. If I win, it's another $2,500."

"Let's go Kathryn," Sarah said and she turned to walk away. "He said if he wins."

"No. Let's hear him out," she said. She pulled her arm free and walked inside. Sarah followed.

"May I pour you ladies a drink?" Camp offered.

"Let's talk about my husband's situation first," she said.

"I assume by your actions that you do indeed have the money I mentioned?" he questioned.

"Not with me," she said. "But I do have the money. The bigger question is can you win the case?"

"I believe I can."

"How?" she asked. "How will you persuade a jury of parents that my husband isn't just another hot-tempered Irishman who killed a young boy?"

"I won't," he said.

"What did you say?" Sarah asked.

"I said I won't try to persuade a jury your husband is innocent."

"Kathryn, let's go. He is a drunk," Sarah exclaimed and stood up.

"I don't understand," she said. "How can you win if you don't convince them he's innocent?"

"There won't be a jury," the attorney announced.

"What?"

"No jury in the world, filled with mothers and fathers, would ever set your husband free," Camp explained. "Maybe they'd go for manslaughter, but probably not. But, let me present my case to a judge who can appreciate the finer points of the law and I have a good chance to win the case."

"No jury? Never heard of it," Sarah scoffed.

"It's called a bench trial and most prosecuting attorneys hate it in a criminal case," he explained. "Old man Barr couldn't pull it off. Neither can the rest of these fools who claim to be criminal attorneys. Hell, all they try are corporate law cases. I'm the only one in Butte with years of courtroom experience."

"Will you guarantee me Sam won't go to prison?"

"No, I will not," Camp replied. "But I will promise you he won't hang."

The three of them sat in silence for several moments before Kathryn said, "I'll give you your $500 now, but only $1,500 when you win the case."

"Madam, I do not negotiate my fee," he said. "If you want the best, then you must pay for it."

"Don't do it Kathryn. He'll just lie to you," Sarah said. "He'll take your $500 and use it to buy his whiskey."

"Mr. Camp," she began, ignoring Sarah's comment. "My father was a colonel in the U.S. Cavalry. He gave me a Colt .45 revolver for my 16th birthday. It's at my house this very minute and I assure you I know how to use it. If, after today, you take one drink before my husband's trial is over, I will shoot you dead where I find you."

"Does that mean we have a verbal contract?" he asked.

"Yes. Now let's have that drink you offered earlier. It'll be your last for some time."

CHAPTER THIRTY-TWO

She lay curled up and wide-awake on a cot next to her son's bed, trying to will him to get stronger. Her eyes moved back and forth from his head to his toes. She longed to hold him in her arms and rock him and tell him everything was going to be all right. And yet, part of her was glad she couldn't, because it was probably a lie. And she hadn't lied to him since the day they boarded the Santa Fe train in Fresno, California, four years ago. That was the day an 11-year-old James had asked his parents if everything was going to be all right in Montana, and they each said yes. It was a lie.

Around eight o'clock the next morning, Doctor Nelson entered the room. He was quiet and his actions smooth and deliberate. After a quick check of her son, he glanced over at her, smiled and said, "The swelling has gone down even more."

"Does that mean he's going to be all right?" she asked.

"Kathryn, we've already talked about this," he said. "It's only been 12 hours and until he wakes up, we won't know if there was any damage to his brain. His speech. His motor skills."

"What did you say Doctor Nelson?" Sarah asked. She and Jessie had been sleeping at the foot of the bed on some old cotton blankets the orderly brought in around midnight.

"I was telling Kathryn, the swelling has already gone down in less than 12 hours," he answered. "But, as we talked about yesterday, we'll still have to wait until he wakes up to see how he's doing."

"Did you speak with the doctor in Billings after the operation?" Sarah asked. She stood and move closer to him and the head of Jimmy's bed opposite Kathryn.

"Why, yes. Yes, I did."

"What did you tell him?"

"I'm sorry young lady, that's between Doctor Radnitz and myself," he said. His tone was clearly indignant.

"Is he coming?" she asked. "Is he coming to see Jimmy?"

"No, he is not coming. There's no reason for him to come," Doctor Nelson replied. "The operation was a success. The boy's still alive."

"Really? Then why isn't Jimmy awake?" Sarah asked.

Doctor Nelson turned away from her and faced Kathryn and said, "I need to make my rounds. I'll check back in around noon." He did not wait for any response and hurried through the doorway.

"Sarah, that was uncalled for," she said. "Doctor Nelson has done everything he can to help save Jimmy's life. You can't talk to him that way."

"I'm not sorry, Kathryn. To him, Jimmy's just another patient. A patient he gets to practice on."

"I don't believe that for one minute," she replied.

"I'm not so sure," Sarah said. "When was the last time you heard him call Jimmy by his name, instead of "the boy"?"

"Doctors don't like to use names," she corrected. "Especially when it's a life or death situation."

"I don't like it. I don't like it one bit," Sarah shouted.

"You don't like what?" Jimmy asked. His voice was hoarse and scratchy.

"Jimmy!" Sarah screamed. "Oh, Jimmy." She reached out and took his left hand in her two hands. His smile was almost imperceptible.

He moved his head slightly towards Sarah and his smile broadened. Then he asked, "Mother, what happened?"

"We'll talk about it later my dear," she replied. "Just close those eyes and let your body regain its strength."

"Jimmy? It's me, Jessie."

"Well, hello little sister," he said. "Don't worry, your big brother is gonna be just fine."

"I'm going to get Doctor Nelson," Sarah announced and rushed out the door.

Jessie moved up to the head of the bed and grasped his hand in hers and asked, "Are you in any pain, Jimmy?"

"Nope. But I am a little tired," he said and closed his eyes.

Doctor Nelson entered the room and approached the bed where Jessie had been standing. He leaned over and said, "Jimmy. Can you hear me? Jimmy? Can you..."

"Can't a guy get some rest around here?" he said and smiled.

"Jimmy, can you count to ten?" Doctor Nelson asked.

"Yes. Can you?" he quipped. "One, two, three, four. That enough doctor?"

"Yes, that's enough for now," the doctor replied. "You can go back to sleep."

As soon as he closed his eyes, Doctor Nelson inspected the bandages around Jimmy's head and chest and then used his stethoscope to listen to his heart. He then looked straight at Sarah and said, "He's doing very well."

"Thank you, Doctor Nelson," Sarah said as she took his hand in hers and shook it.

Then he turned back to Kathryn and said, "You know, it's too soon to predict a complete recovery."

"Yes, doctor."

"And yet, with his remarkable progress, I am willing to venture an educated guess he'll be up an around in less than two weeks. His ribs will be sore enough to keep him from doing anything strenuous."

"God bless you, Doctor," she said. "I know what courage it took for you to operate on my son."

"My actions pale when compared to the dilemma you and your husband had to face," Doctor Nelson said.

She knew this victory celebration would be short lived. In less than 12 hours, her husband would go in front of a judge and begin a fight for his life. And he'd do it with a man whose character was questionable at best. Would the court allow Clayton Camp to take over his case from Robert Barr? Would the judge allow a bench trial? Would the charge be manslaughter or murder? So many questions and possible outcomes, she chose instead to be grateful for the miracle that had saved her son.

CHAPTER THIRTY-THREE

His second night in jail was worse than the first. The tiny cell, the stagnant, putrid hot air was so bad he had to fight back the continual urge to vomit. And that was only part of his torment. What he guessed had been every hour or so, two men would come down and either douse him with two large wooden buckets of filthy, soapy water, or they'd open his cell and kick and punch him. Of course, they never struck his face, telling him, "you gots to look purdy for the judge."

Then, as the rays of sunlight filtered through the dust and dirt covered window at the far end of the room, the door at the top of the stairs opened and Sam prepared for the next assault. Instead, someone shouted, "O'Brien, your attorney is here." As the man walked down the steps, he could hear some men upstairs laughing and saying something about a drunk and a murderer making a good pair.

"Good morning, Mr. O'Brien. My name is Clayton Camp. Your wife has hired me as your attorney."

"Do you know how my son is doing?" he asked. "These bastards won't tell me a thing."

"I'm sorry, I don't," Clayton answered. "But your wife will be in court this morning. You can ask her then."

"I thought some old guy named Barr was going to be here," he said to the tall, slender, middle-aged man in what looked like a slightly worn brown suit and dingy white shirt.

"Once your wife hired me, I called Barr to let him know he was off the hook. I will officially replace him this morning at your arraignment," Camp replied.

"You related to my son's teacher?"

"Dorothy is indeed my sister."

"I've heard about you," he said. "You're a drunk and you live off your sister's income."

"I am a drunk and I do live with my sister," Clayton answered. "I assure you, I do not live off my sister's meager earnings as a school teacher. And the home is mine."

"You're still a drunk."

"Sir, that is a charge I cannot deny," Camp said. "However, it seems I am also the finest criminal attorney in Butte that you can afford."

"How much are we paying you?"

"Sir, I do not discuss monetary issues with anyone other than the person who hires me."

"How do I know you won't be drunk tomorrow?"

"I have promised your wife I will refrain from consuming any alcohol during your trial," Clayton said. "I may be a drunk, but I am an honorable drunk."

"Come closer and breathe on me," he instructed.

"Is that absolutely necessary?" Clayton asked.

"If I'm going to place my life in your hands, yes, "he said. "In fact, for the next few weeks, we'll start each meeting with that small ceremony."

Clayton stepped up next to the bars and blew into Sam's face. Then he said, "I'd be surprised if you could smell anything other than this wretched room."

"What do we do now?" he asked.

"We go to the court and make a plea of not guilty, due to a defense of another."

"Will that work?" he asked. "Will they let me go because I was trying to save my son's life?"

"That's the plan," Clayton said.

"If I was on a jury, I'd let me go," he said.

"There will be no jury," he corrected. "But let's not get into that right now. We only have an hour or so and I need to know everything that happened that morning."

"I was working at the Parrot Mine down at the twenty-five- hundred-foot level when the shift boss told me there was an important message up top," he began. "So, I took the express lift and went up. Sarah was waiting at the top and told me about the fight."

"When and where did you get the pickaxe?" Clayton asked.

"I think it was already on my belt when I got the message."

"Are you sure you didn't pick it up and take it with you?"

"No. But whether I had it on my belt or it was on the ground, I wouldn't have taken a step without it. No one does. It can save your life."

"Then what?"

"Soon as she told me this fight was serious, I took off running."

"Does your son fight often?" Clayton asked.

"I guess so," he said.

"Have you ever seen him fight?"

"No."

"So why go to this one?"

"Because this was the first time I had heard he was fighting a killer," he said. "Sarah told me it was the same kid that killed James' best friend the week before."

"Why didn't you just grab the kid and stop him from hitting your son?" Clayton asked.

"As I ran through the crowd, I heard someone yell, 'He's gonna kill him'" he said. "Then, when I saw him getting ready to hit James again, I just reacted."

"That's enough for now. Let's try to clean you up a bit before we go to court," Clayton said. "Why are your clothes wet?"

"Part of this hotel's first-class service," he joked.

CHAPTER THIRTY-FOUR

The sheriff's deputies were on either side, jerking him along the short walk from the jail to the courthouse. His hands were handcuffed in front of him and his ankles were manacled so close he had to hop to keep up. Clayton had loaned him a comb for his hair and a handkerchief for the blood and filth on his face. As they turned the last corner, he was shocked to see so many people standing at the doorway and out into the street.

"What the hell are all those people doing here?" he asked.

"Well, hell, pardner, you're front page news," a deputy said. "Folks round here love a good hanging."

"I'm sorry, but we're about to disappoint them," Clayton shouted over the noise of the mob.

The deputies pushed him through the people and into a packed courtroom. They slammed him into one of two chairs at the table on the left, facing the judge's bench. He turned and scanned the people crammed together on the wooded benches, already fanning themselves to fight back the heat, and the smell.

"Back here, Sam," said his wife.

He turned around to his wife, Jessie, Sarah and the Sordinos squeezed together in the first row behind his table. When he instinctively reached for her, a deputy standing at the end of his table used a long club to slap his arm back down.

"No contact, scum," he yelled.

"Sorry Sam, I should have warned you," Clayton said.

He was still facing Kathryn and quickly asked, "How's our son?"

"He's going to live, Sam," she replied. "Doctor Nelson did the operation and he saved our son's life. He says James will be very sore as the ribs heal, but he should back up and walking around in a couple weeks."

"If I believed in Him, I'd surely thank the Lord," he said, looking up at the ceiling.

"I believe in Him enough for the both of us," his wife replied.

"All rise. Hear ye, hear ye. Let those with business before this court come forth and be heard by the Honorable Horace Dowell," the clerk of the court announced.

After a few moments, the door in the back of the courtroom swung open and a large man, clearly overweight for his short stature, with shiny black hair, thick glasses, and a handlebar mustache, slowly shuffled towards his weathered, leather chair.

"Please be seated," said the judge.

"In this fifth district court of Montana, at nine o'clock Tuesday morning on the third day of August 1920, Judge Horace Dowell, presiding in the indictment of one Samuel James O'Brien, pertaining to the death of one, Mason Napeel Gillette, on Saturday, July 31st, 1920, with the charge of murder, in the first degree. How does the defendant plead?" the clerk asked.

He and his attorney stood, and then he said, "Not guilty."

"Are there any motions to be made before we proceed?" the judge asked.

"Yes, Your Honor," Clayton said. "The defense moves for a change of venue to the fourth district court in Missoula."

"Denied," replied the judge. "Any other motions?"

"Your honor, the defendant waives his right to a jury trial and asks you to hear his case on Monday, September 20th."

"Does the prosecution agree?" asked the judge.

"We do, Your Honor," answered John Wesley Bunker, Butte's district attorney for the past eight years.

"Wait. I'm sorry, but I can't do it," said the judge as he stared down at desk.

Jumping to his feet, Clayton protested, "With all due respect, Your Honor, if the prosecutor agrees, you cannot deny this motion."

"I have no problem with your motion for a bench trial," the judge began. "It's just that I go to Canada every September for some wild goose hunting. Besides, from the sound of things, I believe this will be a short trial. You have until Monday, August 23rd to prepare your case."

"That's less than three weeks to prepare a defense for a charge of first degree murder," his attorney exclaimed. "It can't be done."

"How about you, Mr. Bunker?" the judge asked.

"We're ready to go to trial today, Your Honor," Bunker proclaimed. "Three weeks or three months, Mr. O'Brien will be just as guilty."

"We'll let the evidence decide that if you don't mind," the judge scolded. "Then the date is set. Any further motions?"

"Yes, Your Honor. The defense requests a change of cell at the sheriff's office," his attorney said.

"I do not run the jail, Mr. Camp," the judge replied. "That said why are you making such a request?"

"Your Honor, the jail has several available cells on the main level. Instead, they've placed my client, who is innocent until proven guilty, below ground in an inhuman environment. It is clearly a case of cruel and unusual punishment that is meant to humiliate and punish my client before he has his day in court."

"So moved. Sheriff Johansen, get that man to the main floor upon his return," the judge instructed.

"Yes, Your Honor," Johansen replied.

The judge stood, banged his gavel and announced, "Court adjourned."

He tried to turn and say something to Kathryn, but the two deputies already had him by the arms and jerked him from his seat. As they pushed and pulled him towards the back door, his attorney said, "I need to talk with Kathryn for a minute and then I'll be over to see you and make sure you get moved."

In his new cell, on the main floor at the back of the jail, Sam collapsed onto his cot and tried to make sense of what had happened. He couldn't. Just as he couldn't help feeling a sense of anger and betrayal towards James. He knew his son loved him, that was an absolute. So why did he lie and go do the one thing he had begged him not to do? Why would he risk his life and now, maybe his father's life? For what? For revenge? For honor? He couldn't understand. At least not yet.

CHAPTER THIRTY-FIVE

The courtroom had cleared except for Camp, Kathryn, Jessie, and Sarah.

"I have a young law student who works for me during the summer and helps with my paperwork," he said. "His name is Matthew Hester. I need you to round up anyone who was involved with this incident, whether they were there at the scene or not, and take them to my office tomorrow and Wednesday and let them tell him their stories."

"I can do that," Kathryn said. "But, what about Jimmy? He'll be in the hospital for at least a week. Maybe two. When will you talk to him?"

"I'll talk to him just before the trial," he answered. "In the meantime, I'm going to the university up in Missoula for the rest of the week. I have some colleagues there who can and will help us with our defense."

"What else can I do?" Kathryn asked.

"I know I don't have to ask this, but I will. Make sure you go see Sam every day," he said. "Twice a day if you can find the time. Jessie and Sarah too. This kind of traumatic event does strange things to people. Even people we think are far too strong to let anything bother them. People like Sam."

"I already spoke with the hospital about my job at the laundry," Kathryn said. "They told me I could take as much time as I needed. They also said I'd have a job as a Practical Nurse when I return. It's not an RN like I was in California, but it's better than the laundry. More money too."

"That's great news, Kathryn," he said. "There's just one more thing we need to talk about. And I need to do it privately."

"Anything you need to say to me, you can say in front of them."

"I truly believe I can win this case," he began. "But even if I don't, I know Sam won't be convicted of first degree murder. That's just a bluff from the district attorney. But you need to consider the possibility of Sam spending some time in prison."

"I'm sorry, Clayton, I can't. I won't," Kathryn said. "Without Sam, we won't survive here. You must win. Now, go do what you need to do and don't bring this up again."

"Matthew will have the telephone number of the dorm where I'll be staying," he said. "I don't know where we'll be working, so if I'm not there, just leave a message with the receptionist, when and where I can reach you and I'll call back."

"Clayton?" Kathryn asked.

"Yes?"

"Are these drinking colleagues?"

"They were until yesterday."

Clayton's life in Butte was no one's business except his sister's. Drunk most of the time, he spent little or no time worrying about his image or reputation. Neither did he care that people assumed he was living with his sister because he couldn't earn a decent living. In fact, he was still wealthy by any standard of the term. He had indeed lost a great deal of money when a certain Alison Stewart, a famous local singer in Sacramento, broke his heart and ruined his life seven years ago. But he had managed to keep more money than his sister could earn in 50 lifetimes of teaching. He was with her because he was her brother. He was with her because she loved him for who he was.

"Camp, you ol' horse thief, you," exclaimed the short, round man with a bald head and a full, grey beard. "How you been?'

"Well, hello Randy," he replied. "Been good as fine wine. How about you?"

"Life is good. The others will be along in a few minutes."

Randolf Berry, Edward Grootendorst and Ronald "Rocky" Taylor had been his classmates at Hastings College of the Law in San Francisco, years earlier. Of the four, only he had a serious desire for fame and fortune. After just a few years of practicing law in California, the other three decided on a life of teaching. They, along with money from his successful practice, helped establish a school of law at Montana State University in 1911. Regardless, they had remained good friends over the years. He had called the same day he took the case.

"Camp, you old bastard," yelled Taylor, as he and Edward entered the room. "How long has it been?"

"Not long enough, Rocky. Not long enough," he quickly answered, and then hugged his friend.

"Clayton, it is good to see you," said Edward.

"Edward. It's always a pleasure to be with you," he said. "Not so with those other two."

"I've arranged for us to take over a small meeting room on third floor of the library," Edward said.

"You mean the Camp Library, don't you?" Rocky interrupted.

"We have little time for your jokes, Ronald," Edward said. "If you weren't such a brilliant researcher, I'd vote to send you off immediately." All four men laughed openly.

"I suggest we begin with drinks at Muldoon's," Randy offered. "Nothing serious, just a few to loosen up the brain cells."

"Sorry boys," he said. "I promised my client and his wife I'd stay off the booze until after the case."

"Jesus, not even a couple?" Rocky said.

"His wife came to my office and offered to hire me if I stayed sober," he began. "Then she explained that her father, who was a colonel in the cavalry, had given her a Colt.45 when she was only 16 years old. Then she looked me straight in the eye and said she'd use it to shoot me dead if I took a drink before this was over."

"Pretty good motivation for giving up the drink for a few weeks," Edward said.

"Back to this case," he said. "Let's start with a poll of who thinks what."

"Manslaughter Two. 10 years at Deer Lodge Prison," Rocky said.

"Manslaughter One. 15-20 years at Deer Lodge," Edward added.

"Not guilty. Defense of Another," Randy said.

"Manslaughter Two. Five to ten at Deer Lodge," he said.

"We clearly need some strategy and precedents if we have any hope of keeping this man out of prison," Edward said. "I propose a schedule from nine in the morning until six at night. We'll be in here when we're not teaching the summer session. Sunday, we'll start with sunrise service and spend the rest of the day fly fishing."

For the next five days, his three colleagues poured over law books, state and local trial records, and even newspapers from the past 10 years. At the same time, he travelled to Billings to interview an old-time friend and mentor, the Honorable Judge William Bare. Rusty, his nickname because of his slightly orange hair, had graduated Summa Cum Laude and number one in his class at Hastings, the same year as he and his three amigos. If anyone could figure a way out of this mess, Rusty could. Unfortunately, he was unable to help during the interview, but he did promise to work on it as much as he could.

At the end of the week, Clayton gathered his notes and dirty laundry and headed back to Butte. They each promised to reconvene the next Monday and continue to search for a miracle.

"Thank you for this," he said. "I couldn't do it without you."

"We know," Randy replied, and then he and the others just smiled.

CHAPTER THIRTY-SIX

Katy had gladly walked the one-mile roundtrip from her home to Clayton's office several times over the past few weeks. She believed solid progress was being made on her husband's defense. The attorney's assistant, Matt Hester, had recorded hours of supporting testimony from the long list of witnesses she had taken there. Clayton had indicated they'd be critical to Sam's defense and it made her feel good to actively help in the process. Today, the Friday before Monday's trial, she was scheduled to meet with Clayton at 9:00 AM to discuss his final strategy.

"Good morning, Mrs. O'Brien," Matt said. "What brings you down here this morning?"

"Good morning, Matt," she replied. "I should ask you the same thing. You don't normally come in this early, do you?'

"No ma'am, not usually," he said. "But Mr. Camp called yesterday afternoon just before closing and said for me to be here before 9 o'clock today."

"Do you know where he is?" she asked. "I have a meeting with him this morning at nine."

"I'm supposed to tell you everything's fine and that he'd see us at the courthouse Monday morning at 8:00 AM," Matt replied. "He, a …," he muttered and glanced down at the ground.

"What is it, Matt?" she asked.

"I'm not certain ma'am, but I think he might have been drinking when he called yesterday," he said. "It was awfully hard to understand him."

"Do you know where he lives?" she asked.

"Yes."

"Take me there."

"Mrs. O'Brien, he'll fire me if I do."

"Young man, I'll shoot you if you don't," she said and pulled a gun from her purse.

"Follow me," Matt said and hurried towards the door. "It's just a couple of blocks from here on Crocker Street."

"Crocker? Did you say Crocker Street?"

"Yes, ma'am," he replied.

"I thought he lived with his sister?"

"He does. But they live in a very large, very nice home," he added. "During the summer, I live there too."

"Is Mrs. Camp home today?" she asked.

"No. When Mr. Camp stopped by the office last Monday on his way back to the university for more research with his colleagues, he said Mrs. Camp would be in Great Falls for the week attending some big teachers' meeting. He said I was on my own until he got back on Thursday night. Then he called yesterday and said he'd see me Monday."

"That's nice," she answered. She wasn't listening as much as she was gawking at the large homes they were passing. She wondered how a teacher and a drunken attorney could ever afford a home in this neighborhood.

"Oh no," Matt said. He had just pushed opened the large, ornate, wrought iron gate in front of Camp's home.

"What is it?" she asked.

"I think we found Mr. Camp."

"Oh, my Lord," she gasped. There was Clayton, eyes closed, jacket on the ground in the flower bed, his white shirt pulled from his pants and his shoes and socks were off. He was propped up against his front door with a whiskey glass in one hand and an empty bottle in the other.

"Mr. Camp? Mr. Camp, are you all right?" Matt asked.

"Well, hello little Matty," Camp stammered. "May I pour you a drink?"

"Oh Lord, what have you done?" she cried.

"Katy? Is that you?" he asked. "May I pour you a drink?"

"You're drunk!" she snapped. "You're drunk when you swore you'd not take a drink until my husband's trial was over. You miserable bastard, why?"

He startled her when he sat straight up and said, "Why? You want to know why I'm stinking, dead-ass drunk? Well, maybe the better question is why aren't you? Your husband is about to be convicted of murder."

"Murder? Murder? What the hell are you talking about?"

"Our great research team up discovered there's no 'not guilty in defense of another' in the fine state of Montana when the person you're trying to save is engaged in an illegal act. And it seems plain old fist fighting is strangely illegal here in Butte. It's not in Great Falls. Not in Missoula. Not even in Anaconda. But here in wonderful Butte, it is. And, we found no other possible strategy that will save him from prison. In short, I have no case."

"So, what are you going to do?" she asked.

"I'm going to stay drunk until Monday morning when the judge will be forced to grant a mistrial. Then you get to find an attorney who won't let you down."

"What makes you think you're gonna live until Monday morning?" she asked and reached into her purse and pulled out her gun.

"You going to shoot me, Kathryn?" he asked. "If not, would you please pour me another drink?"

She stood there staring at the pathetic mess who was her husband's only chance for freedom. Her first instinct was to shoot him dead and walk away. Then she thought she'd shoot him in each hand so he'd never hold a glass again. Finally, she decided it was time to be the adult he chose not to be. She shoved the large gun back into her purse and opened the front door.

"Matt, I'm going to need your help," she said. "We need to get him sober and back to saving my husband. It'll probably take all night."

"I'm your man," he replied. "What's first?"

"A shower. He stinks."

"I'll take him and get him cleaned up right away. I know where everything's kept."

"Good. Show me where the kitchen is and I'll get some food and coffee started," she said. "Can you handle him on your own?"

"Yes ma'am. I've done this before."

CHAPTER THIRTY-SEVEN

One of the benefits of being a drunk was the quick recovery time from each drinking binge. Today, at just before noon, Clayton could barely say a full sentence. By six o'clock that evening, he was already sober, bathed, shaved, fed and dressed in one of his favorite suits. He still had no idea how he was going to keep Sam out of prison, but that was still three days away. His immediate challenge was sitting across from him with gun in her purse.

"Kathryn, I truly apologize for my loathsome behavior," he said.

"We don't have time for apologies or self-pity," Kathryn replied. "You have little more than forty-eight hours to plan a defense that will save my husband. Save my family."

"I promise I'll do my best to convince Judge Dowell this case is really about the Gillette boy and his actions. Not Sam's."

"Your best hasn't been very good these past few years, now has it?" Kathryn said.

"No, and I'm sorry," he said.

"What about your sister?" Kathryn asked. "Do you realize how embarrassing it is for her, a respected school teacher, to live in a town where your actions put you in the same class as the thugs, bums and hustlers that hang out on the south side? If you were my brother, I'd disown you, publicly."

He sat there for a minute thinking of some reasonable reply and then it hit him. "Kathryn, say that again?"

"You heard me the first time."

"No. What did you say you'd do if you were my sister?"

"I'd disown you, in front of a crowd, in downtown Butte at noon on a workday," she embellished.

He stood up, straightened his tie and announced, "Matt. Kathryn. I want to thank you for your help today. You are welcome to remain here, but I need to return to my office."

"Clayton, perhaps I was a little…" Kathryn began.

"No, you were right in what you said. I've been a disgrace to my sister and I need to own up to that," he replied. "But, what I was yesterday does not guarantee I'll be the same tomorrow. I shall see the two of you Monday morning at eight o'clock sharp in front of the court house."

"Clayton, what's going on here?" Katy asked.

"Love, Kathryn. Love is going on here And more importantly, it's going on in Anaconda."

"All rise. Hear ye, hear ye, hear ye. Let those with business before this court come forth and be heard by the Honorable Horace Dowell," announced the clerk of the court as the judge entered the courtroom. "Please be seated."

"Is the defense ready, Mr. Camp?" the judge asked.

"We are, Your Honor," he replied.

"Is the State ready, Mr. Bunker?"

"We are, Your Honor."

"Gentlemen, since I'm hearing this case without a jury, we will forego the traditional opening statements," announced the judge. "And, while I will remain faithful to the full letter of the law, we'll also skip most of the formalities required when a jury is present. Mr. Bunker, you may proceed."

"If the defense will agree to stipulate Mr. Samuel O'Brien did in fact throw a pickaxe into the back of Mason Napeel Gillette's skull at its base, causing instant death, then we can avoid calling some 25 witnesses to attest to that act," Bunker said.

"So stipulated," Clayton replied quickly.

"Your Honor, with that fact in evidence and a full, voluntary confession from the defendant, the State rests its case."

"Mr. Camp, you may proceed," Dowell said.

"Your Honor, my client pleads not guilty, in defense of another, and asks for an immediate verdict of not guilty."

"Denied," the judge announced sternly. "You may proceed."

"Your Honor, this case is about intent," he began. "It's not about the legality of a fist fight between two young boys. It's not about who threw the first punch, the second punch or why. This case is strictly about Mason Gillette's obvious intention at-the-moment just before his death. He was clearly going to kill James O'Brien."

"Objection, Your Honor," Bunker shouted.

"Sustained," said the judge. "Mr. Camp, neither you, nor Mr. Bunker, nor your client, nor even me, can pretend to know what was going through the victim's mind in the last few moments of his fight with James O'Brien."

"Your Honor, Mr. Gillette's public displays the days, weeks and months prior to the fight, leave absolutely no room for interpretation," he replied. "He was going to kill that boy."

"Objection, Your Honor," Bunker shouted again. "Mason Gillette's past has absolutely no bearing on a case in which he was baited into a fight and where his opponent threw the first punch. Those actions, Your Honor, were premeditated and clearly nullifies Samuel O'Brien's plea of, not guilty, in defense of another. Neither he, nor anyone else, can defend a person during the commission of a criminal act."

"Your objection is sustained," said the judge. "Furthermore, this court agrees with your point of law concerning Mr. O'Brien's defense motion. No such plea will be allowed in this case."

"Your Honor, Mr. Gillette was notorious for taunting his victims into throwing the first punch and then using the letter of the law to protect him while he beat his opponents into total submission," he argued. "In fact, Mr. Gillette had already used his powerful, deadly fists to kill twice before. The second time, only a week before, where his victim was the best friend of Mr. O'Brien's son."

"Objection. Objection. Objection," Bunker shouted as he jumped to his feet. "Your Honor, Mr. Camp knows he cannot bring prior events into this courtroom."

"Sustained," snapped the judge. "Mr. Camp, your theatrics may have worked for you in California, but here in little old Butte, you're out of order. Now, do you have anything else to offer this court before I put an end to this farce of a trial?"

"I apologize for my actions, Your Honor, and ask the court's indulgence one last time," he offered humbly. Then he turned and motioned for a small framed woman, with short dark hair and a black shawl wrapped around her to come to the stand. She had been sitting at the end of the front row, just behind Sam's table.

"And who is this?" the judge asked.

"Marie Claudine Gillette," he answered. "She's Mason Gillette's mother."

"Objection!" Bunker shouted. "I have no such person on the defense's initial disclosure list. In fact, I have no list."

"Overruled," Dowell said. "Mr. Camp, please continue."

"Once again, I apologize to the court and to Mr. Bunker," he said. "Mrs. Gillette was only discovered late yesterday afternoon in Anaconda. There was no time to notify the district attorney or anyone else."

"Are you calling Mrs. Gillette as a defense witness?" asked the judged.

"Not at this time, Your Honor," he replied. "I'm merely asking for opposing counsel to join Mrs. Gillette and me in your chambers for a brief meeting."

"Counselors, in my chambers immediately," the judge instructed. "Bailiff, please escort Mrs. Gillette to my office."

He turned and looked at Kathryn. "Pray," he said softly.

The five of them carefully squeezed into the compact office. "Mrs. Gillette," asked the judge. "What would you like to tell us?"

"Your Honor, I want the record to show I object to this incredible action going any further," Bunker said.

"Shut up, John and let the lady speak," Judge Dowell snapped. "You're in my chambers now and in case you've forgotten, I'm in charge. Now, Mrs. Gillette, please tell us why you're here."

"Your Honor, I loved my son with all my heart," she began. "But he was a bad person. Very bad. From the time when he was just a little boy, maybe four or five years old, when he was so much bigger than the others, he began to bully all the other children. Then, when he was around six or seven, it got even worse."

"I'm sorry, but lots of kids fight when they're young," Dowell said. "That doesn't mean they're bad children."

"It was more than just fighting with the other children, Your Honor," she said. "He was cruel. His father, Jean Louis, loved him very much and tried hard to make him better. He even bought him a little puppy to play with. But, from the very beginning, Mason would hit it and kick it so hard the poor thing would just limp away and try to hide."

"Again, I'm sorry Mrs. Gillette, but children tease and torment their pets all the time," Judge Dowell interrupted. "That just doesn't make them a bad child. Most kids eventually grow out of it."

"A few weeks later he killed the dog with his bare hands," she announced softly.

"How did you know it was him?" Bunker asked.

"He told us at supper when my husband asked him where the dog was," she offered, her voice beginning to break. "He said he was tired of hearing it bark, so he took it to the stream and drowned it." Her face went cold, blank, emotionless.

"Was there more?" Dowell asked.

"Much more. Much worse." She reached into her purse and removed a small, lace hankie and covered her eyes.

"Bailiff, give Mrs. Gillette a glass of water," Dowell ordered.

After a small sip of water, she continued. "The fighting and hurting other children—boys and girls—became so bad over the next year my husband and I decided to try and have another child. We prayed he'd welcome a little brother or sister. Someone for him to protect," she said. "It wasn't an easy decision for us. Mason's birth was very hard on me. He was such a large baby and I am not a big woman. I almost died. Our doctor strongly advised us not to do it. But we were willing to try anything to help save our son." She stopped and drank some water.

"I know this is hard," Clayton whispered. "Please, take your time."

"I was in my fifth month and things with my son were only getting worse, instead of better," she said. "His father finally had to spank him for hurting a young girl who had asked if she could help me do some of my chores around the cabin. The next day...," she stopped and drank the rest of the water. "The next day, I was going to see my doctor at noon when Mason pushed me down off our front porch and then smiled at me. I begged him to help, but he just walked away. Jean Louis found me when he came home from work. I lost the baby that night."

"My God," gasped Judge Dowell.

"I'm so sorry, Mrs. Gillette," District Attorney Bunker offered.

"My son has taken three lives, Mr. Camp," she said. "Not two, like you mentioned in the courtroom. I loved him with all my heart. But, if he was still alive, others would die. I wasn't there. I didn't see him. But I promise you, he was going to kill Mr. O'Brien's son. Please do not make things worse by punishing this man for saving his son's life."

Silence hung over the room for several moments before Judge Dowell said, "I cannot know the pain you have endured to come here and share this information. I can only offer my deepest gratitude for your courage and compassion for another human being."

"I apologize for not coming to you sooner, Mr. Camp," she said. "Clearly, I am not very brave."

"Not true, Mrs. Gillette. Judge Dowell is absolutely right," Clayton said. "None of us will ever know the pain you have gone through to help Mr. O'Brien. Thank you."

"May I go home now?" she asked. "It's a long train ride and I'm not feeling very good."

"Bailiff, see to it Mrs. Gillette is taken back to Anaconda in the mayor's Cadillac," Dowell said.

Once she was gone, Judge Dowell spoke first, "Mr. Bunker, when we return to the courtroom, if I announce a verdict of not guilty, in defense of another under special circumstances, what will be your reaction?"

"Your Honor, I have other more pressing matters awaiting me back at my office," Bunker said. "I do not have any more time to waste on a farce such as this."

"Thank you, John," Clayton said. Then he offered his hand and Bunker shook it.

As Judge Dowell stood and headed for the courtroom, Clayton reached out his hand to Judge Dowell and said, "Thank you, Your Honor. You're doing a good thing here today."

The judge pushed past the hand and muttered, "I'm not so sure. I don't cotton much to letting killers loose on my constituents." Then he hurried past and back towards the courtroom.

CHAPTER THIRTY-EIGHT

James couldn't remember the last time he and his family had been on a picnic. Nor could he remember seeing his parents in bathing suits, doing flips and cannonballs into the water. His sister was laughing so hard she rolled on the ground gasping for air. In the four days since his father's trial, life at the O'Brien house had clearly changed. His father had not yet returned to the mines and his mother had taken a few days off from the laundry. Even his sister had asked Doctor Tom for some time to heal from the recent events. For just a few days, money wasn't the most important part of their lives. And even better, Sarah had been with him from dawn to dark, their bond growing stronger by the minute. *If only Sordi were here.*

The next day, around 10 o'clock, Sarah came to his house.

"Good morning, Sarah," his mother said.

"Good morning, Mrs. O'Brien. Good morning, Mr. O'Brien."

"Where've you been?" he asked. "We've already finished with breakfast."

"I had to catch up on some of my chores," she replied. "Not right, me spending all my time over here and not carrying my share of the load at home. Besides, you seem to be getting better every day."

"I am feeling pretty good this morning," he said smiling from ear to ear. "What does everyone want to do?" he asked, not waiting for any response. "Anyone up for catching some big fat rainbows up at Shaver Lake?"

"Not today, son," his father said solemnly. "Where's Jessie?"

"I'm right here," his sister said, rounding the corner from her sleeping area.

"Everyone, please come sit at the table," his father asked. "I want to talk with you."

"Sarah, would you please come back this afternoon?" his mother asked.

"Sure, Mrs. O'Brien," Sarah replied as she started towards the door.

He quickly reached out and grabbed her hand and announced, "Mother, she's part of this family, too. She can hear whatever father has to say."

"She might as well hear it now, Kathryn," his father said.

"Hear what?" he asked and as he sat down in his usual spot with Sarah next to him.

After everyone was in their place, his father reached over and grabbed his mother's hand and said, "We're going back home to California."

Instantly, Jessie let out a huge "Yippee!" and jumped up from the table and yelled, "We're going home. We're going home. Thank God, we're going home." Then she ran over and gave her mother, and then her father, lots of hugs and kisses.

James just sat there, staring down at the table, unable to speak as a thousand questions ran through his mind. After a few more moments, he looked up at his father and asked, "Why?"

"Who cares?" interrupted his sister, before either parent could answer. Then, she resumed her chanting, turned, and ran out the back door and into their yard.

"Did you really ask why?" his mother asked.

"Yes, I did," he answered. "I want to know why we're leaving now, when we just spent almost every dollar we had saved over the past four years. If we leave now, we'll never have enough money to buy back the farm."

"Your mother and I have decided it's more important to get away from this miserable place than it is to stay and risk everything," his father stately firmly. "We leave on the noon train day-after-tomorrow."

"But if we stay, we can make back the money in just a few more years," he pleaded. "Father, you'll find a new partner and I promise to work even harder selling newspapers. Mother can get her nursing license and Jessie can work more hours for Dr. Tom."

"James, your father and I have decided, and that's final," his mother said and reached for his hand.

"No one asked me," he snapped and pulled away his hand. "No one asked me when we came here and now, no one is asking me if we should leave."

"James, that's enough," his mother said.

"It's not enough," he answered. Then he stood up from the table and started to say something more.

"James, your father has the cough," his mother softly declared.

CHAPTER THIRTY-NINE

James was almost to town before he finally slowed to catch his breath. His mind was racing with all sorts of questions and conflicting feelings. He really had no clear idea why he wanted to stay in a city he had hated for the past four years. Was it Sarah? Was it his friends? Was it Mrs. Camp? Or maybe it was not so much what was here, as it was what was waiting for him back in California. Did he truly want to spend the rest of his life as a farmer?

Lost in his thoughts, he wasn't paying much attention to where he was headed or who was in his way. As he turned the corner onto Main Street he ran right into the back of Mrs. Camp.

"Excuse me, Ma'am," he stammered, not realizing it was his teacher as he backed away.

"Whoa, son," exclaimed her brother as he reached to steady his sister. "Where you headed in such a hurry?"

"Mrs. Camp. I'm so sorry," he stammered. "I wasn't watching where I was going. Are you all right?"

"I'm fine, James," she said, her big smile making him feel a little better. "Let me introduce you to Matt Hester. He's been Clayton's law clerk for the past two summers. He helped with your father's case."

"Much obliged for your help," he said. "Folks call me Skinner." He held out his hand to shake with the young man.

"Pleasure to meet you, Skinner," the boy replied. "Sorry we didn't meet sooner. We might have been friends."

"You going somewhere?" he asked.

"He's headed back to law school in Denver," Mr. Camp answered for him. "It's his second year. When he finally graduates in three more years, he'll have a job waiting for him in the public defender's office in Denver. A colleague of mine has run that department for more than 10 years. He's going to clerk for him until he graduates."

"What's a law clerk?" he asked Hester.

"He's the one who does all the work, while Mr. Camp gets all the glory," Hester said with a smile. "To tell the truth, it's the best job in the world if you want to become a lawyer. You get paid while someone teaches you everything you'll need to know to get your degree."

"Really?" he asked as he turned and looked up at Mr. Camp. "How much does it pay?"

"Room and board and three dollars a day for the entire summer," announced Hester.

"Why do you ask, Mr. O'Brien?" said Mr. Camp.

"Is the job still open?" Skinner asked.

"It's only a summer job and besides, a clerk needs a college degree to qualify," Camp replied.

"Would you consider a slightly less experienced person year-round for room and board and, say, a dollar a day to start?" he asked.

"Maybe," Mr. Camp replied. "Who do you have in mind?"

"Me!" he exclaimed.

"You're just a child, son," Clayton responded. "You're not even in high school."

"Mr. Camp, I realize I'm only 15 years old and just starting high school in the fall," he began. "But, just ask Mrs. Camp if she thinks I could do it."

"James, I have no doubt you could, and would do a good job for my brother," she offered. "But, what about your parents? Taking this job requires many a late night of studying and talking about the law. You'd need to live with us."

"My family's leaving Butte on Friday," he explained. My father has the cough."

"I'm so sorry to hear that," Mrs. Camp quickly replied.

"It's not bad. Not yet."

"Young man, for four years I've listened to my sister talk about you and your love of reading and learning everything you can," Clayton began. "If your parents agree to this plan, then I'd consider bringing you on as the youngest law clerk in the state of Montana."

"Thanks. Got to run now," is all he said. Then he turned and ran back up the hill towards his home.

Instead of his home, he ran to Sarah's and up to the front door. He knocked hard several times and without waiting long, knocked several times mores as he yelled, "Sarah Jane!"

"What's all the commotion?" Mrs. Grigsby asked as she opened the door.

"Sorry, Ma'am," he stammered. "I need to speak with Sarah, right away."

"I thought she was over at your house, with you," she said.

"She was. But I had to run to town on an errand and I thought she'd be here by now," he explained.

"Are you looking for me?" Sarah asked as she walked up behind him.

"Sarah, we need to talk. Now," he blurted out.

"Mother, we'll go sit out in back, if that's all right with you?" Sarah asked.

"Don't be long now. You have chores to do," Mrs. Grigsby replied.

"Sarah, I have great news," he began.

"Didn't sound so great to me," she said.

"I'm not going with them," he announced proudly. "I'm staying here with you."

"You can't stay here with me, you fool."

"I don't mean, live with you and your family," he corrected. "I mean, I'm staying here in Butte."

"I don't understand. How can you do that?" she asked.

"I'm going to work for Mr. Clayton as his law clerk. And, part of the job is, I live with him and Mrs. Camp," he said. "The clerk that helped with my father's trial, Matt Hester, is returning to Denver where he goes to law school. Mr. Clayton got him another job with a lawyer friend of his. He's not coming back to Butte."

"Your parents are going to let you do this?" she asked.

"I'm not going to ask them," he replied, staring at the ground.

"Are you crazy? You're only 15," she snapped.

"It's not like I'm going to live on the streets or in a boarding house with a bunch of miners," he said. "I'll be with a very respectable school teacher and her lawyer brother."

"And just how are you going to make this happen?" she asked.

"I have a plan, but it's better if I don't say anything more right now," he explained. "Please, just be at the train platform by 11:30 on Friday morning."

Sarah paused for a minute, saying nothing, as she stared into his eyes. Then she wrapped her arms around him and squeezed so hard he gasped a little. Then he hugged her too, as they swayed side to side for a few minutes. Finally, they parted slightly and kissed a long, long time.

CHAPTER FORTY

The train jerked a few times before slowly crawling towards the southern mountain range that stood between Butte and Salt Lake City, some 600 miles away. Sitting across from James, she searched her son's eyes for any signs of pain or sorrow, as he was finally forced to let go of Sarah's hand as she walked alongside the railcar. He only smiled back at her.

"I spoke with her mother yesterday and she said Sarah can come visit us at Christmas time," she told her son. He said nothing, but continued to smile and nod his head.

"It was nice of your friends to skip their morning paper sales to come to the house this morning," she added. "Maybe they can come visit you on the farm. We'll have plenty of room."

Her son said nothing.

"Would you like that?" she asked.

He nodded.

Trying to prompt some sort of response, she added, "I think I'll miss the Sordinos most of all. How about you?"

"Mother, I miss Sordi every single day," her son replied as he stared out the train car window.

"Mother?" Jessie interrupted. "May I have the upstairs bedroom at the front of the house?"

"Yes, you may."

"Jimmy, I'm guessing you'll want your old room off the kitchen," she said.

"That'll be fine," he replied, as he stared out the window.

"I can't believe Jake Marthedal is letting us live in our old home as part of your father's job," she announced to no one in particular. "If we had had anyone else as a neighbor and landlord, they'd charge us plenty for such a large home."

"Jake's a good man," her husband replied. "I should have listened to him more when we first started farming. We'd never lost the place if I hadn't been so headstrong."

"That's water under the bridge," she said. "Compared to our recent good fortune, we are truly blessed."

Her son stood and moved out into the aisle. He stared down at her and his father for a few moments without saying a word.

"What is it, Jimmy?" she asked.

"I'm gonna go up to the observation car for a while," he replied. "I hear the mountain pass is something to see."

"We have a long ride ahead of us before we reach Salt Lake," she said. "Come on back when you get hungry and you can have a sandwich or two."

He hesitated a moment longer, as if he was going to say something more, but his sister jumped up and announced to everyone in the car, "We're going home. We're going home."

He smiled, turned, and walked away.

She was lost in thoughts of warm summer nights and fresh baked peach cobblers, when her daughter sat back down across from her and Sam. They'd been riding for more than four hours and she was about to ask her daughter to go find her brother.

Instead, Jessie said, "Mother. Father. Jimmy asked me to give you this after we were past the Southern Slope."

She slowly reached out and took the envelope, asking "What's this? Where's James?"

"He said you're supposed to read the letter."

"Jessie, answer your mother," her husband snapped and sat up straight on the wooden bench.

"He's back in Butte," she answered. "When the train was a few miles outside of town, it slowed to make a sharp bend in the tracks. That's when he handed me the letter and then jumped off. He waved good-bye and headed back to town."

"What? Where? He did what?" she asked.

"Please Mother," her daughter said. "Jimmy said it's all explained in the letter."

"Read the letter, Kathryn," her husband said.

Dear Mother and Father,

I've decided to stay in Butte. I know your first reaction will be to come back and get me, but please read on before you do anything.

I'm guessing you're thinking it's because of Sarah that I've returned to Butte. Well, she's certainly a big part of my decision to stay. Even though we've only known each other a few months, I believe we're destined for a life together. But, only time will tell, and we have plenty of that.

There are really two other—maybe even more important reasons—I need to stay on in Butte. The first is, farming just isn't in my blood like it is in yours. It's true, I love being outdoors and in the mountains, but farming without Sordi is just work. Hard work and lots of it. Day in and day out and it's never done. And in the end, success is almost never a question of how hard you work. It's a question of what will Mother Nature send your way. I don't think I could never be happy working on the farm.

The second reason is probably the real reason I want to stay. There are so many more opportunities and adventures here. Sure, Butte has more than its fair share of drunks, bums and thugs. But it also has some of the state's best schools and teachers. And, it has big business and big banks and all the excitement of a Jack Dempsey fight, or a Will Rogers stage show. It has seen the likes of Teddy Roosevelt and the thrill of a William Jennings Bryant speech. It has great wealth just across the street from tragic death. And it has life. A kind of life I want to be a part of.

I've only lied to you once, and that almost cost me my life. I won't lie now and tell you I'm not afraid and that everything will be just fine. I'm scared to death and worried about the unknown. But I'm more excited about my future than I ever have been.

Mr. Camp has given me a job as his law clerk. It doesn't pay much, but it includes room and board in their big house. And, after seeing what he did for Father, I just might want to become a lawyer. No matter what happens with that, I'll be safe with Mrs. Camp. They'll be expecting to hear from you on Sunday, once you reach the farm in Fowler. Their phone number is Redwood 828.

Please trust my instincts and let me succeed or fail on my own. I think this plan is a good one. If I'm wrong, I'll be home before harvest is over and we'll take it from there. If I'm right, I promise I'll come home for Christmas, and we'll all celebrate this new adventure.

I love you with all my heart,
James Michael O'Brien, Himself

Timothy James Riley was born and raised in a small farming community in central California. His father's sporting goods store was the local gathering place for young and old and all things outdoors: hunting, fishing, golf, tennis, etc. His mother managed a ladies clothing boutique and his sister, Jeannine, went on to have a very successful career in film and television.

Tim's business career spanned more than 45 years in sales and marketing management. He was also president of the local service club, chamber of commerce and the prestigious Far West Equipment Dealers Association, representing more than 400 retail dealerships in seven western states. He finally retired in 2016 to spend more time writing and fly-fishing.

Tim published his first book, a self-help guide titled, "I'm Lettin' Go… But I Ain't Giving Up" in 1998. He and Penny, his wife of more than 51 years, have two grown sons and two beautiful grandchildren. They currently reside near Sacramento, California.

72923114R00116

Made in the USA
Lexington, KY
05 December 2017